FIRST LIGHT

JERRY FARNHAM

Published by the author

Edited by Joanne Allen and Donald Wescott

Cover Art by Morgan Kirkland Maurer

Interior Design by Eric H. Bowen

Body Text set in TeX Gyre Pagella 11 point

ISBN: 979-8-218-71704-9 (Softcover)

Also available from the Author:

ISBN: 979-8-218-71706-3 (Hardcover)

E-Pub version ISBN: 979-821817070

NO AI: No artificial intelligence was used in the writing or marketing of this book (nor any other book in the Red at Night series). The author does not permit this content to be used in the training of AI databases.

Dedication

"IT IS OUR CHOICES, NOT our abilities, that show what we truly are"
-Albus Percival Wulfric Brian Dumbledore (JK Rowling)

"LOVE IS NOT ALL: IT is not meat nor drink
Nor slumber nor a roof against the rain;
Nor yet a floating spar to men that sink
And rise and sink and rise and sink again;
Love can not fill the thickened lung with breath,
Nor clean the blood, nor set the fractured bone;
Yet many a man is making friends with death
Even as I speak, for lack of love alone.
It well may be that in a difficult hour,
Pinned down by pain and moaning for release,
Or nagged by want past resolution's power,
I might be driven to sell your love for peace,
Or trade the memory of this night for food.
It well may be. I do not think I would." - Edna St. Vincent Millay

FIRST LIGHT IS DEDICATED TO my first lights, Michelle Hyson Farnham
and Frederick Leighton Farnham. Sometimes, fewer words do the
best. Love you, Mom and Dad, and thank you.

Also by Jerry Farnham:

Red at Night

Red in the Morning

Foreword

A WORD FROM THE AUTHOR

It sounds cliché to say that here I am again with yet another installment of the *Red at Night* series. I had the idea of doing a prequel about halfway through writing *Red in the Morning*. This book has given me the opportunity to add much more depth to all characters, major or minor.

This book also was a time machine for me. Even though Michael is technically "me," Jack and his skiff brought me back to my days of hauling traps from my *Red at Night*. The cover art was created from a picture of me and my skiff.

Speaking of the cover, that credit goes to my old friend and schoolmate, Morgan Mauer. Morgan, thank you so much; you were awesome to work with, and I look forward to working with you more in the future.

Mark and Joanne, my beta readers, how many times did I say this book was done? Thanks for all your time, opinions, and patience.

To my wife and kids, thanks again for standing behind me on this journey. Love you all!

Jerry Farnham

AN AUTHOR'S NOTE

FOR THIS BOOK, I CHANGED the format a little because there were two very different backgrounds at play. I think by separating them into two parts, it adds to the contrast of both Jack and Melissa's backgrounds and helps fill in the holes of why they do the things they do. You will actually learn more about some of the more minor characters as well. I know there will be moments in this book when you will speak out loud, "That's why ..."

PART ONE
JACK'S STORY

DAMARISCOTTA RIVER
BOOTHBAY HARBOR
HEAD OF THE BAY
EAST BOOTHBAY
LOBSTER COVE
BOOTHBAY HARBOR
CABBAGE ISLAND
LINEKIN BAY
MOUSE ISLAND
SPRUCE POINT
BURNT ISLAND
OCEAN POINT
SOUTHPORT ISLAND
SQUIRREL ISLAND
DAMARISCOVE ISLAND
DAMARISCOVE HARBOR
N
W
E
S

CHAPTER ONE
Russell and Anne

RUSSELL HEARD THE NOON WHISTLE that blasted over Boothbay Harbor, a whistle that was originally a warning for air raids in World War II but was now used to let the town know it was time for lunch. Russell, who had been so busy shucking scallops, had lost track of time and was now feverishly wiping his hands clean and running through the picking and shucking area of what was called "The Freezer."

Maybe this time he would get the nerve to say something; maybe this time he would do something different than just look at her from afar. He came through the door of the checkout area, and the sight of her made him stop in his tracks.

Anne Marie Fletcher stood there on the other side of the counter like she had done so many times before. Her jet-black hair was pulled back in a tight ponytail, accented by a white hairband. She had a strong face, one that suggested she was always on guard, but just as every time he had come through this door, she broke out in a smile. It was a tight smile, as if she was holding it back, and her cheeks seemed to blush a little. All the signs were there; why couldn't he make his mouth work?

"Ah, perfect timing, kid. Why don't you help Ms. Fletcher load this order into the van? Rocktide has a larger order today."

Anne found herself in a conflict of interests. She was a strong and independent woman. She could lift, tug, pull, and work just as hard as any man. But this man, Russell Finn, had been eyeing her for weeks. She figured that maybe he didn't want to say anything in front of his boss. Now, if she conceded to taking help that she didn't need, he may just say something.

She decided to surrender and take the help. She wanted Russell to say something, anything, some hint of interest in her. She watched as he grabbed two of the prepackaged boxes; she knew they weighed almost seventy pounds. He was trying to show off! That was a good sign.

It seemed like a good idea to Russell to grab the two boxes, maybe show off a little bit, but with the blood rushing to all his arm muscles to support the weight, it left little for his brain to think with. All he could think about was, how much further to the van? And please don't let me drop this. He could feel his fingertips starting to ache with the pain of holding the boxes. She followed behind him as they walked out into the cold December air. He grimaced when he saw she didn't have the van doors open; he only had seconds of grip left.

Anne cut around him, putting her box on the ground, and then opened the back doors. Russell slowly set them down in the van as calmly as he could, even though he felt he was going to drop them at any moment. He picked up the box she had set down and put that in as well.

With the blood now in full circulation, he taxed his brain on what he could say to start a conversation. He didn't want to ask about the weather; that would be dumb. It was like spinning on ice; the wheels in his mind were turning, but he could get no traction.

"Well, there you go... all loaded up... um," he said, looking at the van, trying to think of something else to say. Then he thought of something and started to speak, but a voice in the back of his head was screaming, "Noooo," but it was too late; the words had already started, and it was like a train wreck; he had no control.

"Awful big van for a woman to drive."

He wanted to slap himself; of all the ignorant, moronic things to say, he said that.

"I manage it just fine. Have a good day."

He swore she called him an ox as she closed the door. He walked slowly back to the picking and shucking room, stood at his station, and went back to shucking scallops. His best friend, Clive Farrin, was in the station beside him.

"How did it go this time?" Clive asked.

"About as bad as it could." Russell answered, then proceeded to tell Clive what he had said.

"Well... that was numb, and to make matters worse, you will be seeing her again tonight."

"What do you mean? We have the Christmas party tonight."

"Yes, and I asked Gwen to come with me. She asked if she could bring a friend; I asked her who, and she said Anne Fletcher. So, I said, yes."

"Why on earth didn't you tell me that before I went out and made a jackass of myself?"

"You didn't give me a chance; you heard that noon whistle and took off out of here, not to mention I didn't know that you were going to be an idiot."

"What the hell am I supposed to say to her tonight?"

"Well, you could start with maybe trying to convince her that you have an evil, ignorant twin that took your place today."

Russell looked at Clive but didn't say anything. He was perplexed; on one hand, he was thankful he would have a chance to redeem himself; on the other, he was worried that he had already sealed his fate.

The rest of the afternoon was spent getting the place ready for the party. All the picking and shucking tables had been cleaned thoroughly, moved against the walls, and covered with tablecloths. Russell went home and got himself cleaned up and ready for the party. Russell wasn't the type to follow the crowds when it came to style, but he did want to impress Anne. She didn't seem to follow any of the trends either. He wanted to look smart; that was something she would want. He wanted to show her she was not the ignorant dolt he sounded like earlier. "How can I look smarter than I am?" Then he smiled. "I got it; I will stop by Wheeler's Drugstore and grab one."

Russell got in his truck and headed to the party. He made the stop at Wheeler's Drug Store and grabbed a corncob pipe and some tobacco. He usually smoked cigarettes, and he had been thinking about quitting those; the pipe would help him quit, and it would make him look more mature.

He pulled his truck into The Freezer parking area and gave his new pipe a light. He took a big drag from it and thought he was going to choke to death. An older man saw this and laughed.

"You puff a pipe, Sonny, just puff it."

Russell took a much smaller inhale and held the smoke in his mouth for a while. There it was; he could feel himself relaxing already. He walked into the party with a confident stride and puffing away like some dignitary.

Anne stood next to her friend Gwen, who was talking to Clive. She felt like a third wheel now. She looked around at the party. This was her first time coming to one of "The Freezer's" Christmas parties. They were the talk of legend, and now she could see why. Not only was there just about every waterfront business owner here, but the place was decorated like what you would imagine the dance hall at the North Pole would look like.

Each window had the Christmas spray snow on it, and that was garnished by a wreath with a red ribbon. Off in the corner was a Christmas tree decorated with scallop shells with little winter-themed paintings in them. An evergreen garland was hung around the walls where they met the ceiling. Bing Crosby's White Christmas was playing over an old record player in the corner. The white walls and ceiling made for the perfect backdrop. With the smells of spruce mixed with the aroma of the food, it was hard to believe that during the day, this place processed seafood. The whole scene reminded her of Old Fezziwig's shop in A Christmas Carol.

The door made a loud creak and a swooshing sound. Anne had just heard it and looked to see who was coming into the door. It was him, the ox, but as much as she was trying to dislike him, there seemed to be some invisible force pulling her attention to him. He looked taller now; she didn't know if it was because he wasn't carrying anything or something else. She was about to turn her head away when he turned and locked eyes with her. That was the last thing she wanted—a reason for him to come over—but he turned in her direction. She started to gather her defenses; she wanted to be as cold to him as the December air just outside. He had his head tipped down just far enough, so his blue eyes were hidden by the brim of his white fedora hat. When he got closer to her and lifted his head, her defenses melted. His eyes held his apology; she could read it, hear it, and even feel it. He had a sheepish look; he knew he had said the wrong thing, but his grin, after he saw her expression, said that he knew his apology was accepted. In a moment of a look, they had a conversation without a word spoken.

She looked him up and down now. Russell didn't seem to have a sense of style, nor did he seem to care. He had a leather biker jacket on and regular blue jeans, not the bell-bottoms everyone was wearing. He wore a pale, solid blue button-up shirt with the top two buttons undone, as the guys were doing. On his feet were a shiny pair of leather dress shoes with small buckles on the top. The only thing that was really throwing her off was the stupid pipe he had clenched in his teeth, but she might learn to live with it.

Russell grinned the best he could while keeping the pipe in his mouth. He almost regretted having it, but the way she looked at it, he figured she liked it. He figured it must have distracted her from how nervous he probably looked. He wanted to say some type of apology, but it seemed to him there was none needed, like they had come to some type of agreement.

She looked wonderful; her hair was pulled back and had a red bow. It accented the red dress with white trim that she was wearing. She had chosen to go with a Christmas-themed outfit. The dress was form-fitting but not too tight, with a high neckline. She didn't dress like some of the floozies out there. She wore ankle-high black leather boots.

Russell found himself gazing into her warm brown eyes; they had a heat to them, and with the dress, they almost looked red. He could tell there was more smile there than she was showing, like she was holding some of it back, trying not to show how happy or interested she was. He realized by the awkward stare that Gwen and now Clive were giving them that they had been stuck staring at each other for a while. It was now time to speak.

"So, let me start again fresh. My name is Russell, Russell Finn, and you are Anne Fletcher, right?"

"Yes... how do you know my name?" she asked.

Russell hadn't thought this far in advance. How did he say that he saw her during the summer, when he was delivering some lobsters and clams to Cabbage Island, where she worked? She was busy unloading the lobster and clams and putting them on individual trays. He admired the fact that she was working so hard but had a smile on her face and a bounce to her step. She was humming a tune, and it flowed to his ears like warm caramel. Would it sound bad that he immediately asked about her on that day? Or how, when Cabbage Island closed for the season, he was disappointed that he never got a chance to say something to her? Or how his heart nearly jumped from his chest when he saw her walk into the front room of The Freezer to pick up an order for the Rocktide Inn in September. From then on, he would shoot out to the front at noon to try to catch a glimpse of her.

"This summer, I saw you working out on Cabbage Island; I asked who you were."

"And you have been coming out to the front almost every time I come to pick up an order at The Freezer."

"Yes." Russell answered honestly, knowing that it could be the end of this conversation.

"And today, you helped load the van."

"Yes."

"All this time you knew my name but couldn't say hi or ask me out?"

"Anne, there are several important moments that happen in a person's lifetime, moments that will live in their mind forever; no matter if they go good or bad, they will stay with a person for the rest of their lives. I am not going to lie to you, Anne; you wouldn't be the first girl I ever asked out, but something about that first moment I saw you, every moment I have seen you since then, this afternoon and now, makes me think that you... you will be the last girl I will ever ask out, and when I do... I want to get it right."

"I think you just did." She responded.

They spent the rest of the party in each other's arms. If not dancing, they were talking; if not talking, they were laughing. Both were wondering when the moment would arise that they could kiss. Neither of them had realized they had become the topic of conversation for many at the party. They seemed to have a glow about them, a warmth. At the end of the evening, Anne told Gwen that she would be getting a ride home with Russell. Russell had intended to stay behind and help his boss clean up from the party.

"I think you have something more important to tend to, my boy," said his boss, nodding at Anne.

"Yes, sir." Russell said and went and helped Anne into her coat, then opened the door.

After closing the door behind him, he looked over his shoulder and saw that the moon was full and that every wave in the harbor seemed to twinkle, making the harbor seem to magically glitter.

"Anne, I know it's a little cold, but let's walk up here a little." Russell said, wrapping an arm around her side.

They walked together, Anne's boots clicking on the pavement, until they reached the overlook in front of the Catholic church. From this point, you could see the entire inner harbor.

Russell turned and looked into Anne's face. The very tip of her nose and her cheeks were turning red; he wasn't sure if it was the cold or something else. He took a deep breath while trying to think of something to say, but there was nothing to say. They said it all, looking at each other. He bent down and kissed her gently and warmly, and deep down they both knew that this was going to be their last first kiss.

CHAPTER TWO
Kiddos

"Do you, Anne Marie Fletcher, take this man to be your lawfully wedded husband from this day forward— to have and to hold, in good times and bad, for richer or for poorer, in sickness and in health; will you love, honor, and cherish him for as long as you both shall live?" said the preacher.

"I do." Said Anne, with confidence and assertion.

"Do you, Russell Jonathan Finn, take this woman to be your lawfully wedded wife from this day forward— to have and to hold, in good times and bad, for richer or for poorer, in sickness and in health; will you love, honor, and cherish her for as long as you both shall live?" said the preacher.

"I do," said Russell.

"I now pronounce you husband and wife; you may kiss the bride."

Russell stepped forward and gave Anne a kiss; as their lips touched, everyone in the small church erupted in a cheer. They walked out of the church to see that Clive had pulled Russell's nineteen fifty-seven Chevy Bel Air out in front of the church. People had decorated the car with streamers and a sign in the back window with the words "Just Married" painted on it. Russell opened the door for his new wife, then did a "Dukes of Hazzard" slide across the front. He fired up the engine and put the three-speed manual transmission into first gear on the column shift. Anne knew what he was about to do and normally would protest, but not now; she just braced herself while the engine roared and the tires squealed.

After the car had caught traction, Russell let up on the gas pedal and let the car sort of coast. He wanted to take time getting down to MacIntyre Lobster, where the reception was going to be held.

They drove around town getting cheers from bystanders and friendly horn honks from other cars. Anne had slid over and was sitting in the middle of the large bench seat. They decided that everyone had made their way to the reception by now and headed to MacIntyre Lobster. Russell pulled the car in, and he and Anne walked into the restaurant to loud cheering again. They took their seats, and soon everyone else was sitting, eating, and talking.

Clive looked around, and when it looked like everyone had stopped eating, he stood up.

"Anne, I have to tell you, but I am sure you already know this: you have just married one of the most stubborn, thick-headed, and numbest men you could have ever found. Russell doesn't know the meaning of the word quit. He set eyes on you, and he knew he had to have you. You have also found one of the hardest-working, most honest, kindest, and funniest people I know. Treat him well, and he will take care of you. Russell, you found yourself one hell of a woman there; you take care of her, or I will take care of you."

Everyone had a laugh, and the celebration continued. When not on the dance floor, Russell and Anne talked to guests. Russell couldn't keep his eyes from Anne, who had a glow about her. At the end of the party, Anne and Russell walked down the ramp and onto the dock where Russell's boat was tied. He helped her in, and they pulled away from the dock.

"Where are we going, Mr. Finn?"

"Well, Mrs. Finn," he paused for effect. "Over to the cove, then we pack our bags, get in your car, and head to Quebec City just for a couple of days. It's a five-hour drive but through some of the best of Maine."

"What are we going to be doing there?" Anne asked with the most innocent tone she could muster.

"We will start workin' on making a family! You better get some sleep on the way up."

"Oh, don't worry about me, but something tells me we may have to stop along the way. I am not going to wait five hours to make love to my new husband."

Anne wanted to tell him that in that moment there was already a new Finn growing inside her; they had already started the family. With the wedding coming up, she didn't want to tell him. She would tell him tomorrow morning.

NINE MONTHS LATER, RUSSELL SAT in a chair cradling his new baby girl. His wife was asleep, exhausted from the twenty-two hours in labor delivering the nine-pound eleven-ounce human being now sleeping just like her mother, in his arms.

"Hey, little Lucy, you're not so little, are you? You wore Mommy out trying to get you into this world. Let me tell you about her. Your mother is one of the best people on this earth. Now, she may be edgy at first, probably not to you, but most people have to kind of earn their way with her. If you want to grow up and be the best you can be, you just do what she does. Now me, I am your daddy; the lord broke the mold when he made me, I can say that because I have been told that all my life. My job is to provide for you and protect you, and I promise to do just that."

Anne lay there, biting her lip and trying not to cry; if she cried, her body would shake, and Russell would know that she was listening. She didn't want to spoil this moment. She knew long before now Russell would be a good father. She watched him play with the other fisherman's kids down at the dock. She continued to lay there and listen to Russell

"Lucy, your full name is Lucy Anne Finn, Lucy is not short for anything; my boat is named *Lucy*, and since we made you on that boat, we decided it should be your name. Anne is obviously your mom's name, and Finn is our family name. We came over from Ireland over one hundred years ago."

The sun was rising now, and Russell could see it just barely through the shades. He stood up with Lucy snug in his arms and pulled the shades aside. The hospital room looked out over the harbor. The sun was painting the blackish water with highlights of red, orange, and yellow. Russell looked down to see that the light gave Lucy's face a warm glow, like a small fire.

"And that there, Lucy, is Boothbay Harbor. It's the best place in the world to grow up. We have good schools and all sorts of things to do and all kinds of opportunities! You can be whatever you want to be, and I and your mother will be right behind you."

A couple of days later they were released from the hospital; Anne sat in the back of her Ford LTD station wagon; Lucy was fastened in a car seat with Russell at the wheel. What normally would have been a seven-minute ride home took fifteen minutes or more. Russell was driving like there were eggs in the car, and they would all break at the slightest jerk.

Russell had already been home and installed all the special child-safe locks on the cupboard doors and refrigerator and put outlet covers on. He was quite proud of himself for making the house "kid safe," but in just seven months all that effort seemed to be futile. Lucy was crawling around and opening every cupboard. Anne and Russell had to put all the cleaning stuff in the dish cupboard and pack away their good plates and cups; they ended up getting plastic dinnerware and keeping that in the bottom cupboard.

Not long after crawling, Lucy was walking; then came her first words, then the endless questions as the little girl learned about her world. As Lucy learned about her world, Anne and Russell learned about parenting. Russell's constant joke was, "Are you sure there isn't a manual for her somewhere? Maybe we left it at the hospital, or maybe it's..." he learned to stop there.

Lucy was what the doctors called a large-framed girl; she was taller and bigger than all the girls her age and most of the boys. Other than that, she was a healthy and smart child with an angelic smile. Russell's favorite part of the day was walking through the door to get his "Lucy hug." It didn't matter how the day went; it always got better once he picked up his daughter. Russell was always the guest of honor at Lucy's tea parties; he sat in the small chair, keeping his weight on his own bent knees and tired feet, trying not to flatten the toy chairs. He usually sat next to King Big Paws, Lucy's stuffed bear, and Queen Fancy Feet, a ballerina doll. To him the imaginary tea and cupcakes were the best in the world.

Anne came to the door and looked in.

"Lucy, may I borrow your father for a moment?"

"Yes, Momma."

Russell got up slowly and followed Anne into the bedroom; she shut the door behind them.

"Ugh, it's a kind of bad timing for us to be walking in here like this, don't you think?"

She opened the top drawer of her dresser and pulled out a small, white, wand-looking thing; it looked like a thermometer but different. She held it up and saw two thin blue lines.

"Does that mean what I think it means?" Russell said with joy building from deep within.

"Yes, it's not official, but yes, we are pregnant again."

"You, are you sure?"

"Oh yes, very sure."

"Can we tell her?" asked Russell with an almost childlike tone.

"Go ahead."

He left the bedroom and went back down the hall to where he had left the tea party.

"Lucy, we have some news for you." He paused, not knowing how to tell her. "Um, do you remember us telling you how babies are born? Well, your mommy is going to be having a baby; you are going to be a sister!"

Lucy looked at them, then around at the table where her guests were sitting.

"Well, that just messes everything up!" she said in an angry tone.

Anne jumped in. "No, honey, it doesn't mess things up; that means you will soon have someone else to play with."

"I know, Momma, but my tea set is only for four people; I think Dada won't be able to come when the baby gets here."

Dᴜʀɪɴɢ ᴀ ᴄᴏᴏʟ ᴀᴜᴛᴜᴍɴ ᴅᴀʏ, with the trees bright with the colors of fall, Jackson Thomas Finn, Jack for short, was born at St. Andrews Hospital. It was Russell, this time asleep in the chair, while Anne held her new baby boy in her arms.

"Now, Mr. Jack, that man you see over there, the one snoring up a storm, he is your father. I am here to tell you: you have the best father you could possibly ask for. Now as you grow up, you want to do just what he does and do what he says, and you will be a good man, just like he is. Oh, sure, you will probably hear me call him an ox from time to time, but he is a good man, but all good men need a little poke now and then."

Russell was still snoring away, so she slowly slid out of bed and walked to the window. It was a bright and sunny day out, but a stiff nor 'east wind was making the inner harbor have white-capped waves.

"You see that big ole ocean out there? That is where your daddy works; he goes out and hauls lobster traps. It's a dangerous job at times, and even though I act like I am not concerned, I worry every time he leaves the house." She paused and walked back to the bed; the short time on her feet had already made her legs weak.

"Pretty soon here, I imagine your sister is going to come barging in. I have a feeling she is going to take the role of big sister very seriously. She is a good girl though, big for her age. I have to say, I am glad that you were normal-sized."

Almost as if on cue, Lucy came barging into the room, waking up Russell, and vibrating with the anticipation of meeting her new baby brother. Russell's parents had been watching her; they stopped at the door so as not to intrude on the new family.

Lucy stood by the bed while Anne held Jack closer to her.

"Hi Jack, I am your sister, Lucy. I love you."

Anne and Russell smiled at the moment.

"Hey Russell, take Jack for a moment so Lucy can get up here with me."

Anne passed Jack to Russell and helped Lucy up onto the hospital bed. Anne moved the back of the bed a little higher so the two of them could sit up.

"Now, settle in between my legs and lean back against me a little."

As soon as Lucy was settled in, Anne nodded at Russell; Russell knew what Anne was thinking.

"Lucy, put your arms out, like how you carry King Big Paws when he is sick," Russell gently instructed.

Lucy's face beamed as Russell gently laid Jack in her arms. Lucy was half scared of hurting the baby, but that fear was overpowered by love and caring.

Russell now had a tear rolling down his cheek as he gazed at his whole world, sitting in that hospital bed. Anne tipped her head to see her daughter's smiling face.

"Hi, Jack. I am your sister Lucy, your big sister. We are going to be the best of friends. I can't wait until you are old enough to come to one of my tea parties; they are the best."

CHAPTER THREE
Lucy and Jack

It was a bright and shiny day; the sun was out, warming the morning air. This was the perfect day for the start of the new school year. The small family stood outside Boothbay Region Elementary School; Lucy had climbed up into the big circular hole in the concrete just outside the doors. It seemed that the architects had a vision of kids sitting in it and getting a picture taken on their first day of school, like that was its purpose, and that's what it got used for.

"Don't worry, Jack, three more years and you will be coming in too!" said Lucy, hopping out of the circle after Anne had taken the picture. Jack was holding on to his father's leg, hiding his face.

It was no surprise to Anne or Russell that Lucy was ready to get in that school. There wasn't the slightest inclination of fear. She had been talking about it all summer, even practicing by calling her mother Mrs. Finn and having her mother or father play "classroom" with her, using Jack, King Big Paws, and Queen Fancy Feet as other pupils in the class.

There were several other parents there waiting as well, all with other first-time students. The principal, Mrs. Nash, came out and greeted them all and said it was time to start, and she would be escorting them to their classrooms personally.

"Ok, Lucy, time to go." Anne said as she started to bend down to give Lucy a hug, but Lucy had already shot towards Mrs. Nash, her Barbie-doll-themed backpack bouncing on her back. About half the distance away, she stopped and ran back to Jack, who was trying to stay strong, but the tears had overcome him and were trickling down his cheeks. Lucy took her shirt sleeve and wiped away the tears.

"Don't cry; this is a good thing, Jack. I will be home before you know it. I need you to be strong for Momma and Daddy, ok?" She said it as if she were the adult in the group.

Jack nodded, then gave his sister a hug. She then gave both of her parents hugs as if to show them support. She reassured them she would be fine, then took off at a run again to the doors.

Russell picked up Jack and carried him back to the car. Jack had his chin resting on his father's shoulder, looking back at the doors of the school, hoping that Lucy would come popping out of them.

What would he do now? He had spent his days playing with Lucy; they went everywhere together - grocery shopping with Mommy, the library, playgrounds, and sometimes playing at home. Lucy made the best monster truck noises and the best imaginary tea in their kingdom when they played king and queen. Who would run the boat now when they played lobsterman?

Anne found the adjustment hard too. Where two kids entertained each other, one would not. She didn't want to plop him down in front of the TV; that wouldn't do.

"One day at a time, Anne. Just take one day at a time," she told herself.

For Russell, nothing really changed. He would still go lobstering, and lobstering was going well. It gave him an immense sense of pride being able to provide for his family so his wife could stay home and raise their children. His boat, an older Ervin Jones-built wooden boat of which he was the second owner. It was still in good shape, but he knew in a few years he would have to move to something bigger. The new fiberglass boats had been out for a while now, and he had heard good things about them. No more sanding and painting every year; just buff and paint the bottom. They were lighter too, which would save on fuel.

Every day Jack would walk up to the top of the hill and watch Lucy get on the bus. Every afternoon his mother set an alarm, the Lucy alarm, Jack called it, so he would know when to dart up the hill to greet Lucy as she got off the bus.

After three years of waiting for his turn, three years of watching Lucy get on and off the bus, looking at all the schoolwork she brought home, and meeting all the new friends she had made, it was his turn to get his picture taken in the big circle outside of the school. He was much more timid than Lucy.

"Jack, this is the first big step into a long adventure; it's the first challenge," Russell said encouragingly.

Jack was still unsure, not wanting to break from his father's grip. Lucy had come back from the doors and took Jack's hand.

"Come on, Jack, we got this."

Jack loosened his grip on his father's jacket and walked with Lucy into the school. They both looked back when they got to the door and gave a wave to their parents.

With both kids in school now, Anne found herself with excess time on her hands. Russell was still making good money lobstering, so there was no need to worry about working. She was able to make the kids' lunches every morning and then see them off to school. She would volunteer at the school a few days a week. That way, she always had an ear on what was going on at the school.

When winter approached, Anne found herself wishing for snow days as much as the kids did. For her, there was nothing better than watching her two kids play together. Jack and Lucy were very close; sure, they had made some friends in school, but when it was time to plan birthday parties, they always had their sibling first on the guest list. They had their fights, but Anne learned if she didn't always play referee, sometimes just monitoring and watching them work through things themselves was all it took.

As they got older, Lucy's size wasn't necessarily an issue, but it certainly became more noticeable. She was taller and larger-framed than all the girls in her class, as well as most of the boys. Some of the boys had taken to calling her "Lucy the Large" or "Large Lucy." This had its effect on Lucy; she came home crying a couple of times. Jack had caught wind of this, and one afternoon when the boys were chanting their "Lucy the Large" song to Lucy, Jack walked up to one of them, the biggest one, and popped him right in the mouth.

The teacher was so surprised… not only that Jack hit a boy three years older than him but also knocked out one of his teeth and sent the boy off crying - that took a few moments to process. In that short amount of time, Jack had started crying. Partly because he had hurt his hand, cutting it on the boy's teeth, and he was also scared of what was going to happen next.

Mrs. Nash, the principal, had called in Russell, Anne, and the other boy's parents. They all gathered in a conference room; there was confusion and tension in the room. Nobody spoke, but everyone was wondering what was going on.

"We had an incident today, and I thought it would be best if I brought everyone in to get to the bottom of it. Lucy, can you tell me how this started?"

"Yes, I was playing by the monkey bars when that boy," she pointed at the boy with an ice pack on his jaw sitting with his parents, "and his friends started singing 'Lucy the Large' over and over. I asked them to stop, but they didn't; he and his friends followed me, singing that stupid song over and over." Lucy started getting choked up and was fighting to not cry at this point.

The boy's mother had loosened her grip on her son and turned to look at him. "Is this true, Wyatt?"

Wyatt sheepishly nodded his head yes.

Russell stirred in his seat, not sure how he was feeling about this. His heart ached for his daughter, knowing how much this taunting had been hurting her, but when he looked at Wyatt's father, he could see how embarrassed he was and almost pitied him.

"Jack, can you tell us what happened next?" prompted Mrs. Nash.

At first Jack was dead set on staying quiet. What would his father do when he learned he punched another kid? What would Wyatt's father do when he found out Jack was the one who knocked out his kid's tooth?

"Go on, Jack," said Russell. "It's ok; I think we all know what happened, but it would be best if you told us."

Jack wasn't sure how his father knew, but he said to go on, and that is what he had to do. He took a deep breath and started from his first thoughts.

"Well, I see Lucy coming home every day crying. I heard her say she never wanted to go back to school, but I know Lucy loves school, so this boy and his friends were really hurting Lucy's feelings." Jack stopped, being interrupted by a noise coming from Wyatt's mother; she seemed to have a tear rolling down her cheek now and had completely let go of Wyatt. "I didn't think that was right; I figured if I punched the biggest of the boys, they would all stop. So, I jumped up and punched him with everything I had. I didn't mean to hurt him that badly. I started getting scared that I really hurt him, and I would be in trouble."

Mrs. Nash sat, observing both sets of parents in the room; she knew how to deal with this. "I think I will step out of the room for a moment. I believe you parents can sort this out better than I can. I will be just out in the hall if you need me." And she got up and left the room, closing the door behind her.

"Wyatt Brian Conners, you march over to that little girl right now and apologize," his mother demanded.

Wyatt showed no interest in defying his mother's orders. He walked over to Lucy and said, "Sorry."

"No, no, no," that isn't good enough, young man. You say, 'I am sorry I hurt your feelings and will never make fun of you again'."

Wyatt could hardly get the words out, the emotions of the events starting to take hold.

"I think you two boys should shake hands as well; I don't think any apologies are necessary, but a good handshake should set things right." Russell said, nodding at Wyatt's father and getting a nod back.

"Yeah, and Wyatt, from now on, if one of your friends starts making fun of Lucy here, it's your job to make them stop." Wyatt's dad said sternly.

"Yes, Dad."

They filed out of the conference room into the hall, where Mrs. Nash was waiting. "Everything settled?"

Both sets of parents said yes and thanked her for how she handled the situation, and she stood watching as both families walked down the hallway and out the door. Her assistant came out and asked, "No report or discipline, Mrs. Nash?"

"No need for paperwork, and I do believe the discipline has already been taken care of, just as it should."

CHAPTER FOUR
The Lucy J

RUSSELL SAT AT THE KITCHEN table with his tax reports in front of him, with all his records of money made over the previous years. Then he looked at his notes on what it would cost him to finish off a new fiberglass hull on his own. He really liked the looks of the thirty-six-foot Stanley hull; he had called and gotten some rough numbers for a hull and top. He had talked to a local Cummins Marine Diesel dealer to get a price on an engine. He had added some additional costs to the estimate and had come up with a number on how much it would cost to step into a new boat next season.

Looking at all this information, he felt if lobstering kept going like it had been going, he could make the leap. It was a big leap, but doable. The voice of his father echoed in his head, though: "Don't count your chickens before they hatch" and "When your plan involves an 'if,' it's not a plan, it's a gamble."

Several guys in the harbor had already gone to the newer fiberglass hulls; more than half of the fleet was fiberglass now. He and Anne had talked it over, and she had said, "If you think you can do it, then go for it." There was that "if" word again. He was just about to put the paperwork away when he decided to grab the phone and call the bank.

"Hello, First National Bank of Damariscotta, Brenda Blackman speaking."

"Hi Brenda, this is Russell Finn. I want to set up an appointment to talk to someone in the loan department. I think it's time for a new boat."

"Ok, Russell, how about tomorrow afternoon?"

"That will work for me."

"See you then."

"Thank you."

Russell hung up the phone and leaned back, staring at the paperwork in front of him.

"There, if the bank approves it, then I am going for it."

The next day, right after Russell left the bank, he called the John Williams Boat Company and found himself talking to Jock Williams himself. He ordered his new hull and sent the deposit check that same day. With the next call he had ordered the engine; then it would be a waiting game until the hull arrived. He could have gone with a bigger engine; his best friend Clive and Jock both tried to talk him into a 3208 Caterpillar marine engine at three hundred and seventy-five horsepower, but Russell was a fan of the Cummins engine and had heard good things about them. He told Clive he would get an Isuzu or an Iveco before he put a Caterpillar in his boat.

Russell constructed a large bow shed, also known as a Stimson bow roof shed, in his front yard. Using two pieces of strapping with blocks in between them, they are screwed together in an arch form. These arches are leaned against each other to form a large, almost bullet-shaped frame. Russell built two dozen frames and stood them up two feet apart and used extra strapping to cross-brace between the frames for added strength. This made his bow shed forty-eight feet long, with the bow of his arches a width of 16 feet. This would give him plenty of room to work on the new boat and leave him room for a work area off the boat. He then had a local shrink-wrap company apply clear shrink wrap to the outside of the framing, leaving the ends open. This way the truck would be able to drive in, set the boat down, and then drive out. He would then build rigid ends to the shed with a door and a wood stove for heat, along with adding a couple of "torpedo heaters." To do fiberglass work, the shed would have to be warm, and he would also have to set up some type of ventilation system.

Two months later, Russell took delivery of the engine, and then two days before Christmas, the big black hull showed up. Russell had Skip Rideout come with his boom truck to put the engine in before it was pulled into the shed.

After Christmas, he built walls at both ends; one end had a door, and he built a chimney out of stovepipe. He made sure the outlet of the chimney was far from the shrink wrap so as not to start a fire. He put box fans at the top of each wall to help ventilation and hung a tarp from the ceiling to catch all condensation that would drip from the shrink wrap.

The beginning of the new year brought the beginning of Russell working on the boat. He started with the engine placement. Building himself a small gantry, he and

Clive were able to get the engine hanging in its final place. From there Russell had Lee Sheldon make up engine brackets that would tie the engine to the boat. Lee would also be the one to make the davit and any other brackets or parts that needed to be fabricated.

With the engine location figured out, it was time to start working on the deck. He had Jock Williams put a floor flange in while laying up the hull. A floor flange is nothing more than a tap sticking out from the inside of the hull; it leaves a place for whoever is finishing off the boat to tie the deck into the hull.

Jack, who was now five years old, was very interested in what was going on. If there was ever a moment when Anne couldn't find Jack, he was out in the shed helping his father. Jack would pass screws to Russell, and even though the added step did slow Russell down, he enjoyed having his son next to him, being a part of the boat that would provide for them all.

After the deck had been built and covered with fiberglass, it was time to start building the cabin top and rails. Like the deck, everything was built with pressure-treated, marine-grade lumber and plywood, then fiberglassed over.

Fiberglass is a three-part construction system: you had the resin, normally a polyester type; a hardener that acted as a catalyst to make the resin harden; and then the mat or cloth. The area to be fiberglassed would be lightly sanded with coarse sandpaper; this would give the surface "tooth," as some people said, for the resin to attach to. This would all be wiped down with acetone to ensure a clean mating surface. Sheets of mat or cloth would be pre-cut and laid out, then set aside in the order they would be needed. Then the resin and hardener would be mixed, the ratio dictated by the temperature and humidity in the environment. After the resin was mixed, the area would be wetted out with the mixed resin, and then the pieces of mat or cloth would be laid out. Then the mat or cloth would be wetted as well until no dry spots were visible. A hard roller dipped in acetone was used to work out any remaining air bubbles.

The process was often intense as you were racing against the clock, trying to complete it before the resin began to harden. You were also wearing a mask with air filters that made communication a struggle and added to the intensity. Even with Russell's ventilation system, after fiberglassing, nobody could work in the shed, so they saved it for the last part of the day.

After the deck and house were completed and all major structural work was done, it was time to work on the details and subsystems. Russell had hired Martin Knapp to do his electrical work, while Lonnie's Hydraulics took care of the steering and trap hauler. Russell built a single bunk in the forward cabin, along with some storage shelves for odds and ends.

He used white oak for all the toe and combing rails. He knew the best thing to do was to paint them, but he just couldn't bring himself to cover up the oak. So, he called Carroll Lowell, who was well known for boat building. Carroll tried to talk him into painting the oak but then gave him a secret recipe of Coopernol mixed with linseed oil and thinned with turpentine. Instead of stainless-steel half-round trim, he opted for bronze to give the boat a warm feeling. He knew he was getting a little...yachty with the boat, but it was much more than a boat to him.

Lobstermen tend to think of their boats as some type of living being. Not only did the boat get called a "she," but it was also the means of how they fed their family, how they provided, very much an extension of themselves. Memories were made on lobster boats, first fish were caught, lessons were taught, and generational knowledge was passed down. The lobster boat was a tool, a classroom, a play area, and a friend.

The boat was finished in late March; now it was just a waiting game until the ground would be hard enough to drive the truck across. Russell had started a rule that nobody was allowed in the shed until launch day. He had the name put on and wanted it to be a surprise. He got it all washed up and buffed the hull to the point he could almost shave looking at the side of the hull.

After a good long warm spell, the ground had dried out enough that Russell had the truck driver come and check it out. The truck driver walked around the yard and gave Russell the thumbs up

"Saturday morning, I will be here. Can you get that end opened up?" asked the truck driver.

"Sure can," answered Russell.

Saturday morning came, and Russell had gotten the word out. All the local fishermen had showed up to check out the new vessel. As the truck backed in, Russell and Clive took the last two screws out of the end and the front wall.

"Anne, you and the kids close your eyes."

Anne did as he requested, and so did Lucy and Jack.

Russell and Clive worked a couple of pry bars around, and the wall fell free with a thump. A group of bystanders grabbed the wall and dragged it off to the side. The truck backed the trailer in, and in a few short moments the trailer had the boat off the jack stands and was holding the boat.

Anne, Lucy, and Jack still had their eyes covered; it felt like hours had gone by, and Anne started to feel a little foolish. She could hear the truck pull ahead and the gasps and whistles of the onlookers.

"Stop for a second!" Russell hollered to the truck driver.

The truck driver stopped, and then Russell hollered again, "Open your eyes!"

It looked too good to be a lobster boat to Anne; it looked like one of the lobster yachts many of the summer people had. The white top was gleaming and reflected the sunlight. All the woodwork looked golden and warm, like she could snuggle up to it. The black hull reflected every blade of grass. Even the red bottom paint seemed to have a warmth to it, but what grabbed Anne the most, tugged at her core, and almost made her shed a tear of joy among these strangers was the name. Up on the bow and across the stern in gold lettering was "*Lucy J.*"

"What do you think, Anne?" Russell asked.

Anne had to swallow and compose herself so her voice wouldn't crack when answering. "It's beautiful, Russell, just beautiful."

"Lucy, look, it's your name!" said Jack

"Jack I was going to put *Lucy Jack*, but *Lucy J* just sounded better; you ok with that?"

"Yes, Daddy, Lucy is a good big sister; she deserves to have a boat named after her."

The truck driver started moving again and heading out of the driveway. Russell told all the onlookers that they would be launching the boat at Murray Hill over in East Boothbay, then coming back here to the dock for the launching party.

CHAPTER FIVE
New Sternman

RUSSELL COULD JUST BARELY HEAR the engine as his boat went out of sight; it was gone, taken away. He kept looking out at Lobster Cove, like the boat would disregard the stranger at the helm and come back to its true owner, but it didn't. He took in a deep breath to fortify himself and slowly and shakily exhaled. He walked up the ramp to the dock house and went inside, his emotions building up pressure. He went to the old fridge to find no beer in it, then closed the door, almost slamming it shut. He checked his cupboard to find a bottle of Glenfiddich twelve with just a couple of ounces left in it. He sighed in relief and set the bottle on his bench. There was a mason jar of hog rings just an arm's reach away. He could dump out the hog rings, wipe out the jar with a rag, and use it for a glass. As he reached for the jar, he knocked over the bottle; when it hit the floor, it shattered.

His eyes stared at the broken bits of glass and the splatter of scotch, then focused on an oak runner. The one-inch by inch-and-a-half, rough-sawn, four-foot piece of oak, which normally would be attached to the bottom of a lobster trap, now looked like an outlet to Russell—a weapon against the walls that had closed in on him, a weapon against the misfortune of last summer's fishing season, a weapon against his own ego, trying to be one of the "big guys" and taking a much too large of a step, only to fall, to fail.

He picked up the runner in his strong, calloused hands, cocked the runner back over his shoulder, much like a baseball player would, and swung with every bit of strength he had at the refrigerator that didn't have a beer for him. It left a dent across the door, but that wasn't enough for Russell; he had crossed his threshold of patience and reserve, and that one swing felt so good. He continued to swing at anything he could find, sending nails, screws, and paint cans in multiple directions.

Anne stood outside the dock house until the storm was over, not only for her safety but also for Russell's benefit. He needed to do this. He had kept his head up, strong and positive for her and the kids. He needed to fall apart. He did the same thing when his father died: stayed strong for his mother, taking care of everything. Then Anne saw him sitting on the dock, crying to his father that he wasn't ready for him to go. Russell was a strong man and a good one, but all men fall, and it's the wife's job to help them back up.

He had swung away all the anger; he was now sweaty, and his hands were bloody from the rough wood. He picked up his old favorite stool, the back of it now missing, being a victim of his temper; he stood it back up and sat down. He placed his hands on top of the other at the end of the runner, and with the other end on the concrete floor to bear the weight, rested his head on his hands and stared down at the floor, watching the tears and sweat drip off of his face and mix on the cold floor.

He knew—he knew just what he had done wrong. He counted his eggs before they hatched, something his father had warned him about. But the year before last's lobstering had been so good, and he had saved so much money, he thought he would be all set.

He beamed with pride at the launching party. He had done it; he was one of the "big guys" now, with a new boat and new traps, and was thinking about buying a new truck, a fancy three-quarter-ton diesel, with a plow maybe. His wife, Anne, came down to the boat and sat with him. She told him she had arranged for a babysitter for the kids, then opened the companionway door and headed for the forward cabin of the boat. They spent that night on the *Lucy J.*

That would be the only good memory he would have on that boat. That summer the bluefish were rampant, causing the pogies (menhaden), the lobstermen's prime choice of bait, to form tight schools in which they would suffocate with the lack of oxygen in the water. The dead pogies washed up on the shore up and down the coast of Maine, killing the tourist season; no tourists meant no demand for lobster, driving the price down. With all the pogies dying, there were few left for bait, driving up the cost of bait, if there was any bait at all. On top of this, the fish that eventually sank to the bottom kept the lobsters fed; there was no need for them to crawl into traps when there was free food littering the bottom.

Russell would normally have a little financial cushion going into winter, but with the dead summer and a break-even fall, he felt his back was against the wall going into winter. He was getting behind in his payments, and he was pushing the safety envelope with the weather he was going out in, taking risks on days he really shouldn't have gone out. He had even sold his precious Chevy Bel Air. But when spring came around, the writing was on the wall. He spoke to the bank and arranged a voluntary repossession for the boat and truck.

His thoughts were interrupted by the squeak of the hinges on the dock house door, announcing Anne's entrance. Russell picked up his head to see Anne coming into the dock house, walking cautiously so as not to step into any wet paint or onto a nail.

"You must be ashamed of me; look what I have done to us." Russell said in a grizzly, solemn voice.

"Russell Kirkpatrick Finn, I am not ashamed of you yet. It's what you do next that will make up my mind on that. The Russell Finn I know, the one I married, the one that is the father to my children, and the man I love, will wake up tomorrow and start the next chapter."

Russell stared at his wife. How could she not be ashamed? How could she still have faith in him? Didn't she see his failure? She could; she knew he had failed, but she also knew that he wasn't the kind to roll over. She knew he wouldn't quit, and she knew he would take care of his family no matter what. He didn't know what the next chapter would be yet, but he was confident Anne would stand behind him. He stood slowly, using the runner to steady himself; he turned towards his wife and walked towards her. She took his bloody, splintered hands into hers.

"Let's go patch these up. I will talk to Big Tom in the morning to see if they need any help in the restaurant this summer. That way, this won't be on your shoulders alone, and I don't want to hear a word about it; you can stow the Finn pride."

The next morning, Russell decided not to go down to the dock; he didn't feel like socializing with his peers. There was a part of him that felt he was no longer their peer. They had boats; he had lost his. He also knew that any one of them would let him borrow their boat, but he wasn't in the mood for charity. He wanted to start the fight; he would buy a small boat and keep hauling traps; he would save his money, pinching every penny. He went to Grover's Hardware store and bought an Uncle Henry's, a book of used items people had for sale in the Maine, New Hampshire, Vermont, and Massachusetts area. He went home and started looking for a small boat to haul out of.

After circling the ones he could afford, he got on the phone and started making phone calls. He kept this process up for a couple of weeks. Anne gave him all her tip money from the restaurant. Soon a twenty-foot Eastporter that Anne and Russell named *Tip Jar* was tied up at Russell's dock. It was about as basic as you could get—no seats, steering wheel, or controls. A simple outboard with a PVC pipe as an extension on the tiller. Russell built a trap deck to put traps on and installed a pump for keeping lobsters alive. At first, it was tough to go out and haul traps in a twenty-foot skiff while his friends, the people he grew up with, still had their full-size boats, but Russell was on a mission to take care of his family and to move forward. He would be back in a full-size boat again, but he would have to work for it. On days that Anne wasn't at the restaurant, she would help him on the boat.

On the day school went out for the summer, Anne and Russell decided to splurge a little and take Lucy and Jack to the movies. In the movie, there were kids riding around on dirt bikes. Lucy could have cared less about them, but Jack came out of the movie theater making engine noises and acting like he was on a dirt bike.

That evening Russell had just put Jack to bed when Jack asked, "Daddy, can I have a dirt bike?"

Russell's knee-jerk reaction was to say "no," but before his mouth could open, his brain caught up.

"Sure, Jack, we start looking into it tomorrow morning. Get some sleep; you're going to need it."

Russell closed the bedroom door and sat down in his recliner in the living room. Anne had the TV on but wasn't watching it; she was more involved in her crossword puzzle in the Boothbay Register.

"Anne," said Russell as he turned the TV to the evening news; he wanted to be sure the weather was going to be good the next day.

"Yes, Russell," she said, not breaking her attention to the crossword puzzle.

"Pack a second lunch for tomorrow; Jack is going with me." He settled back in his chair and watched the news. As he sat there, he started second-guessing his decision: did he really want to drag his son into this life? He had just lost his own boat and put his family in a difficult spot; the industry had no certainties other than change, and that wasn't always good. Jack was only six; who was to say that he would stick with it? He might just be like a lot of the other kids and go sternman until the end of high school, then take off for college, or be like that Michael Williams kid and join the military. There was no harm in him working for a while as a sternman.

The next morning, Russell woke his son up softly. Jack got himself dressed and sleepily met his father in the kitchen. "Are we going to go get my dirt bike, Daddy?"

"Nope, we are getting you a work ethic; you can use that to get your dirt bike." Jack was unsure of what was going on; he was still quite sleepy; he just knew somehow this was leading to a dirt bike.

The walk down to the dock had woken Jack up enough that he was figuring out what was going on. "Daddy? Are you taking me lobstering with you?"

"Sure am! And I am going to pay you, too! I will start you off at ten dollars a day; if you save your money, you can buy that dirt bike you want by the end of summer." Russell looked over his shoulder to find a large grin on Jack's face.

Jack loved this plan. Not only would he get to spend time with his dad and go out in the boat every day, but he would also earn money and buy his own dirt bike. He decided to run up ahead and start doing whatever he needed to do. Once in the boat, Russell showed him how to put the fish on the bait iron. He explained to Jack it was his job to keep the irons full for the next trap and to keep his area of the boat clean. Russell took a spare five-gallon bucket and turned it upside down for Jack to sit on. He untied the boat, and off they went. Jack went to work, stabbing two fish in the eyes with one bait iron, then the other, so two irons were ready to go at all times. Bait irons were nothing more than an oversized needle, sixteen inches long and the same diameter as a pencil, with the tip flattened and a hole in it for threading a bait line through. There was a simple wooden handle on the other side. Jack was warned to mind the sharp tip and always have it pointed down in the bait tray. As soon as Russell would put an empty bait iron back, Jack would put two more fish on it. Russell could see his son was taking his job very seriously and, at the same time, was taking in the environment around him.

Jack's world now had expanded; he had been out in the boat before, but now he felt like he was part of the ocean. He could smell it, hear it, and almost taste it when he drew in a deep breath. He wasn't just a spectator; he was in the game. He focused on his work first, making sure the bait irons were not only ready but positioned in a way that his father could grab them with ease. Soon he started looking around, and then the curiosity of the new world started nagging at him. He saw other boats, islands, and seagulls.

"Whatcha lookin at, boy?" His father asked.

"Everything, Daddy, there is so much to see out here."

"Yes, there is, boy; yes, there is. Don't you hesitate to ask a question. This is your world, Jack. It belongs to you as much as you belong to it," said Russell, clenching the pipe between his teeth.

"Well, where are we, Daddy?"

Russell chuckled at the question; it was simple and fair. "We are on what is called the Spruceful Shore, just outside of Lobster Cove. You know Lobster Cove, right?"

"Yes, that is where we live."

"That is right! We are on the west side of Linekin Bay, in the general area of Boothbay Harbor, in the Atlantic Ocean."

"Wow, the Atlantic Ocean; that's big, isn't it, Daddy?"

"Very big, Jack, you see that island way out there?" Russell pointed outside of Linekin Bay. "That is Squirrel Island; if you go fifty miles or so past that, then turn east, you could end up in England, Spain, or Africa."

Jack stared out towards Squirrel Island, the world seeming bigger and smaller at the same time. He had seen these places before on the globe at his grandparents' house. But on the small globe, they seemed so far away; now he realized he was on the same ocean as those distant countries were on. Russell smiled, looking at the wonder on his son's face. "What a gift," he thought to himself.

The day went on with Jack asking more questions; Russell had to limit him to one question per trap. To keep him more occupied, he had Jack start banding the lobsters as well and told him he would be getting twelve dollars a day with the added responsibility. The dirt bike was still the goal, and Jack certainly liked the idea of getting paid and having a job. But this started to be something different. He was out on the water with his father, just the two of them. He didn't have to share his time with Lucy or even his mother. "This is going to be an awesome summer," Jack thought to himself.

CHAPTER SIX
Stephanie Ann Turner

Ten years later, Russell Finn looked over the bow of his new, but used, boat, *Wicked*. So much had changed in ten years. Russell had worked his way out of *Tip Jar* into an older twenty-six-foot wooden lobster boat that he fished for a few years. Then, he spotted the ad for this boat and decided to upgrade again to a thirty-foot South Shore lobster boat with a three hundred and thirty horsepower gasoline engine, a "Chevy 454," as it was called. Russell had bought it from a fellow in Harpswell that raced more than he lobstered, but the boat was for a good price, and if he saved his money, he could put a diesel engine in over the winter.

Over the water, Russell could see a red skiff headed for him, bouncing from wave top to wave top. His son showed no fear being in such a chop in a twelve-foot skiff. Normally, Jack would be out lobstering with him, but today, Russell was just moving a few traps around. Jack decided to use the day off to haul through his own traps. The red skiff came alongside. Jack ducked under the snatch block that was hanging from the davit and grabbed onto the wash rail. Russell peeked into the boat and saw that Jack already had a tray full of lobsters.

"Well, it looks like you are nailing them today," said Russell, resting his hands on the straps of his oilskin overalls and clenching his pipe between his teeth.

"Yeah, that hotspot we found over at the Elbow, I doubled my gear there and am nailing them."

Russell shook his head in disappointment. "Jack, do you know what you have done? You just told everyone that fishes in Linekin Bay that there is a hotspot there. Everyone knows you fish with me, and we hauled through there yesterday, and then you go and hammer the area. That's not smart. You are showing our cards."

Jack's face contorted as he thought through what his father had just said. Russell could see that his son was troubled that he had disappointed him.

"Jack, this is an easy fix, and you don't have to go moving your traps out of there; you can hide them."

"Hide them?"

"Everyone out here knows you fish singles, right, so go back through and rig them as pairs; that way you double your gear, and nobody knows. Just make sure you tuck those extra buoys under cover so nobody sees what you are doing."

"That is a slick idea."

"Yup, and remember the next time you haul them to only have one on the rail at a time. How much do you have left today?"

"I am getting wetter than a Taco Bell fart with this wind stirring up the chop; it also has me drifting all over the place as soon as I get the trap off the bottom. I have twelve traps between Tumbler Island and Clam Rock and another ten around Harbor Island; those spots will keep me in the lee of the wind. If the wind dies down, I will keep going; if it doesn't, I will be right close to the dock so I can sell."

"Sounds like a smart plan; your VHF is on, right?"

"Yes, Dad, and I don't have my stereo cranked up too loud either. I have heard enough of Jane Watson to last a lifetime."

"I know what you mean; at first it was nice, but now her voice is like nails on a chalkboard."

"Or, like you and Mom asking me if my homework is done or if my room is clean."

"Boy, I will slap you with a pogie for that!"

"Have to catch me first!" Jack twisted the throttle of the outboard, and the two-stroke motor launched the skiff forward, soon skipping across the wave tops while Jack stood, maintaining balance like a surfer.

Jack had gone sternman with him every summer since that year he wanted to get a dirt bike. It wasn't just earning the money, though; Jack had a love for the water and working on it. The state of Maine allowed people as young as twelve to get a lobster license, and as soon as Jack was twelve, he had it filled out, all by himself, including addressing the envelope, putting the stamp on, and even getting a money order for the registration fee. Jack bought an old plywood skiff from his father; Russell had used it for clamming. Jack decided to paint it red, with a black stripe along the waterline and gray bottom paint. He had seen a plaque in a dragger that his father worked on that said, "Red at Night, Sailors' Delight, Red in the Morning, Sailors take Warning". That would be the name, *Red at Night*.

He also found an old, small, five-and-a-half-horsepower Johnson outboard. That was fine for Jack's first season, but he wanted to go a little faster, so the next season, he went a little bigger and bought a twenty-five-horsepower outboard. Two years after that, he bought a brand-new forty-five horsepower Yamaha and was one of the fastest skiffs in the area.

Jack had about one hundred traps of his own, divided between Linekin Bay and inner Boothbay Harbor. He had been hauling since five o'clock in the morning and taking a beating from the wind all day. He ate his lunch on his way over to Tumbler Island; today's lunch was an egg salad sandwich, his favorite. He cracked open a Dr. Pepper and set a rag over it to keep the salt spray out of it. He saw one of his buoys coming up, white with a Newport green top and pink spindle. He grabbed the buoy by hand—no need for a gaff in a skiff—and started hauling the trap by hand, placing the rope in a neat pile just to the side of him.

Out of the wind, his skiff didn't drift away so much when the trap was lifted off the bottom. With a few more pulls of rope, the trap broke the surface, yielding five or six lobsters flapping about in the trap. Jack turned the trap on his trap deck and opened the door. With his lobster measure, a piece of bronze with two sides, one for the minimum size and one for the maximum size, he checked each lobster for legal size, checked the tail for a v-notch, and checked if there were any eggs on it.

"That's three for me," he said out loud. Then he baited the trap and closed the door. He put the outboard in gear, grabbed the PVC pipe he had on the tiller handle to extend it a little, and spun the skiff around, looking at his small Furuno GPS/Fish Finder. He looked at the readout at the bottom and pushed the trap into the water. The twelve traps he had in this area rendered the same results: two to three lobsters per trap. Now it was time to shoot over to Harbor Island. The wind had seemed to die down so he could continue to haul the rest of his traps. He looked around the harbor to survey the boat traffic. "Hhhmmm, still pretty quiet... I can haul around Harbor Island; that will put me at around two o'clock. I still have an hour before she gets out of work...unless I take my time. Yeah, I got to get this t-shirt off and roll these oilskins down."

He ended his internal monologue and took off his T-shirt; it was wet anyway. Then he rolled down his overalls to look more like pants, exposing his tanned upper half. He hauled his traps around Harbor Island slowly, taking his time. He had timed it perfectly; the summer girl from Squirrel Island and a friend were walking down to the Tugboat dock. She kept a small Boston Whaler there. She was working at the Tugboat Inn, cleaning the rooms. He had talked to her a little last time she was headed back out to the island. Her blonde hair was pulled back in a ponytail, and Jack could only imagine what it would look like if it was let down. She had on a navy-blue Tugboat Inn polo shirt and tight white shorts. She reminded him of Kelly on that show 90210. He decided to motor over and talk.

"Hey, I didn't get your name last time I saw you here," Jack said, standing as tall as he could.

"My name is Jessica; you can call me Jess. What is your name?" She slightly blushed.

"My name is Jack." He couldn't think of anything else to say to keep the conversation going.

"Jack, Jack Finn, is that you?" Her friend spoke up.

"Yeah, do I know you?"

"We had science class together with Mrs. Hersom, first period on gold days."

"Oh, yeah, Stacy, right?"

"No, Stephanie, Stephanie Turner," said Stephanie, slightly annoyed. She had seen Jack around for years. Boothbay Harbor is a small town, and the school was just as small; she was sure he knew who she was; he was just playing coy or some other game because of Jess. Jess was her friend, so she didn't make a big deal about it.

There was an awkward silence as the three of them tried to figure out what to do. Stephanie decided to help her friend out.

"Hey Jack, we are going to her house on Squirrel Island, then headed into Barrett's Park to hang out on the beach. Would you like to meet us there?"

"Sure, why not the beach on Squirrel?"

"Too cold, and too many parents; my dad doesn't approve of my bikini," said Jess.

Jack had to focus, and the vision in his head was making that difficult. "Okay... ah... I will go in to sell my lobsters and meet you guys over there."

He spun the boat around and headed to MacIntyre Lobster. He had to remember he was in the inner harbor, and it was a no-wake zone. Once at MacIntyre's, he sold his lobster; it was a Friday, which meant he would get paid for all the lobster he landed that week. While heading out of the harbor, he cleaned up his boat, took off his oilskins and boots, and put on his Crocs. He turned his Boothbay Seahawks hat backwards, and as he passed the five-mile-per-hour buoy on the way out of the harbor, he said out loud to himself. "Time to haul ass!" He opened up the throttle, and the skiff skipped across the light chop like a stone.

"*Red at Night*, come back. Jack, that you I see sliding along Spruce Point?"

Jack recognized the voice. It was his shop teacher and his father's best friend, Clive Farrin.

"Yeah, it's me, Mr. Farrin."

"You got your scuba mask with you? I just sucked something into the wheel. Can you come cut it out?"

"Damn it," Jack said out loud but not into the radio microphone. He didn't want to miss his chance with Jessica, but Clive always paid good, and he knew he was one of the lobstermen that set aside extra bait for him and the other kids that fished out of MacIntyre's. He looked over the horizon to see if he could see him while lifting the microphone back to his mouth.

"Yup, whereabouts are ya, Mr. Farrin?"

"I am over here on the north side of Card Cove at Ocean Point."

"I will be over in a few minutes."

Jack throttled back up and headed to Clive; now, none of the students ever called Clive by his first name, even during the summer. He was Mr. Farrin until you graduated, and then some. Jack was already wearing shorts; he removed his wallet and tucked it away. He knew Mr. Farrin would have a knife ready. He coiled up his bow line and grabbed his scuba mask from storage. Jack approached the boat from astern, cut the engine, and tossed his bow line to Mr. Farrin's sternman. He removed his hat, placing it on the tiller arm of his outboard, put on his mask, and then kicked off his Crocs. He stood up on his trap deck and leaped into the air, doing a somersault into the water. He popped back up to the surface.

"Holy shit, that is cold!" Jack said excitedly.

"If we were in shop class, I would give you a sweeping detail for that, Jack," said Clive jokingly.

"If we were in shop class, you wouldn't have rope in your wheel, Mr. Farrin."

"You do have a point; I am some glad to be out of that classroom. Here is a knife. Be careful; I have a cage there, but something must have drifted in."

Jack took the knife and a large breath and went underwater.

The ocean in Maine is nowhere as clear as it is in other places in the world. It's a murky green color, and the visibility is between ten feet and the length of your arm, depending on where you are. Jack positioned himself with one hand holding the rudder. The trick was to keep yourself calm and relaxed so you wouldn't use so much oxygen. Clive did have a cage, a metal grill of sorts around the front of the propeller. It was supposed to prevent rope from getting in the wheel, but sometimes someone would back into some rope. In this case, it looked like a piece of float rope had floated into the cage, then got wound up as soon as Mr. Farrin put the boat in gear.

There are a few rules Jack followed when diving on someone's propeller. First, the engine had to be off. Second, there had to be at least one person topside. Third and most important: never try to slide your hands through the rungs of a cage; cut from the back. There were two lines leading from the propeller to the cage. One line was drifting to the surface while the other was headed to the bottom. He decided to cut those two lines and tie them back together, then go up for another breath. He popped his head back up at the surface.

"You had some float rope in your wheel; I think it's from that five-trapper over on Ocean Point. I cut him free of it. Now I will go down and cut it from your prop." Jack took another deep breath, and down he went.

It always made Clive nervous how long Jack could stay underwater just by holding his breath. The seconds seemed like minutes, and it always seemed too long. Clive was starting to get nervous when Jack popped up again with a large ball of float rope.

"Christ, Jack, do you have gills or something? I was getting nervous for a second there."

Jack chuckled while catching his breath. "You are all set now. Someone needs to talk to that five-trapper about using float rope. Not to mention he has twenty fathoms of rope when he only needs twelve."

The cold was starting to set into Jack; any longer and he wouldn't be able to get back into his boat. He swam over to his skiff and pulled himself onboard. Out here, the water was much colder than up in Barrett's Park.

"Jack, I don't have any cash on me; are you going to be going to MacIntyre's tonight with your folks?"

"I suppose so."

"Alright, I will catch you there then."

"Sounds good, Mr. Farrin!"

Jack spun his boat around and headed for Barrett's Park.

Stephanie sat on the rock wall of Barrett's Park, watching a small rock crab crawl across the muddy bottom. She and Jess had worked this out. Jess was just here for the summer; there was no reason to get tied up with a local boy, just to leave at the end of summer. Stephanie had been interested in Jack all last school year, so Jess dropped Stephanie off at Barrett's, knowing that Jack would come back. And knowing Jack was a nice boy, he would give her a ride back to Boothbay Harbor. She was thinking she may have to walk back to the Harbor for her mother to pick her up, but then came the sound of Jack's boat. The sound of the outboard at full throttle was decorated with the washing of water that the hull passed over. The closer he got, the more nervous she got. Would he be so disappointed with Jess's absence that he would just leave? That wasn't Jack, though; she had observed him during the school year. He wasn't just funny; he was kind.

At the end of the school year dance, he had asked one of the girls from the special education class to dance with him. It wasn't a gag or a cruel prank.

The poor girl and her other friends from the special education class had been sitting in a corner, just watching. Jack walked over, stuck out his hand, and brought one girl out onto the dance floor. It started a movement of sorts; other students started asking the others to dance as well. Jack Finn, a freshman, changed the way Boothbay Region High School students looked at the special ed class. It wasn't love at first sight, but it was an interest and confidence knowing that this boy would be a good man. She wanted to see it firsthand; she wanted to be a part of it, even for a short time, as young love often is.

"Where is Jess?" he asked, bringing Stephanie back to the present.

"Oh, uh. She couldn't stay. It looks like you have already been swimming."

"Yeah, Mr. Farrin sucked in a big ball of rope and called me on the radio to help him out."

"You have a radio in there?"

"Yes, I have a VHF for talking to other boats, and I also have a stereo."

"Nice, look, I know you came here looking for Jess, but I am here. If you want, I will swim with you, but if you don't, I understand, but either way, would you mind running me back to the harbor? My parents are supposed to be picking me up at five."

"Well, I already got my swimming in; how do you feel about a boat ride?"

"Sure, where to?"

"It's not too choppy; we have just enough time to run out to Ram Island and Fisherman's."

"That sounds like fun."

Jack helped Stephanie into his boat and placed the hoodie he was wearing that morning on the trap deck so she had a cushion and so her bottom wouldn't get too wet. He sat down beside her and headed out of Linekin Bay. Her black hair was braided in a ponytail, which kept it from flying in his face, but he could still smell the scent of her shampoo; the smell of apples was just enough to overpower the ocean smell. He was happy he didn't get any bait while he was at the dock. She was wearing a light blue swimsuit with loose-fitting black gym shorts. She was holding on to what was either a large purse or a small bag. With every little wave he hit, she seemed to slide closer to him. Soon, he was holding both of them from sliding back. He tightened his grip on the trap deck with his right hand. Jess was now a distant memory. He knew of Stephanie; he even considered asking her to one of the dances during the school year, but the timing never seemed right. "Well, funny how that worked out," he thought to himself.

Once at Ram Island, he slowed down so he could idle up to the rocky beach. Jack shut the outboard off and tipped it up so the propeller was no longer in the water. He moved around Stephanie and grabbed an anchor that seemed to have two lines coming off it, then she noticed it was one line passing through a hoop. Instead of asking, she decided to observe. The boat still had a lot of momentum going, and Jack quickly tied off one end of the anchor line to his boat. He dropped the anchor in the water, letting the line feed out until the boat gently rubbed on the rocky beach. Jack put one foot on the beach and kept the other in the boat to hold it still. He then held out an arm for Stephanie. Once off the boat, Jack pulled the line, and the *Red at Night* went gently out away from shore. As he watched the boat, he looked down to see a piece of blue sea glass. "If this goes well, I will give her that to remember this day by," he thought to himself, then reached down and picked it up and put it in his pocket.

"That is a neat trick," Stephanie said, observing the simple maritime engineering and wondering what he had just put in his pocket.

"It's called an outhaul, so I don't have to worry about the tide beaching the boat. I will just run this end up and tie it off to something."

"Do you come out here often?"

"Yeah, I come out here and pick up buoys and traps washed up on the shore; the guys pay me around one dollar per buoy found."

Stephanie looked at her surroundings; there were some white clapboard buildings with red shingled roofs and a small bridge that led out to a lighthouse. They walked to the center of the island, staying clear of the houses. Jack explained that people lived there, and he liked to give them their privacy. Jack pointed out all the other surrounding islands. He went on to say that he and the *Red at Night* had been on almost all of them. She envied his freedom; he left his parents' dock early in the morning; he hauled his own traps and made his own money. Now he had changed his plan and was out here on this island with her. She had to be back at a certain time.

"Jack, what about your parents? Don't they worry about you out here, all by yourself?"

"I called my dad on the VHF after leaving Mr. Farrin's boat. I told him I would meet them at MacIntyre Lobster for dinner later. Just about every lobsterman in the harbor knows me and the *Red at Night*; I have babysitters all over the place."

They walked around a little more until Jack mentioned if they left now, he could run easy back to the harbor and have a more comfortable ride; also, they could turn on the stereo. The ride to the island hadn't been rough for Stephanie, but she liked the idea of a slower ride. The outboard had been loud; she was hoping they could talk.

Once headed back to the harbor, Jack started wondering. He had never asked Stephanie if she had a boyfriend. He didn't remember if she had one last year, and it didn't seem to him she would be here sitting so close to him if she did. He wanted to open that door, though, plant that seed, and let her know he was thinking in that direction.

"So, um, Stephanie... are you... I mean, do you have a... um?"

"No, I don't have a boyfriend. Yes, I like you. When will you ask me out?"

"Ahh, now, I guess. I am not doing anything tomorrow. What are you up to?"

"I am working at the Ice Cream Factory until five tomorrow."

"Uh...ok....um...." Jack was stumbling to keep up and figure out what to say next.

"Listen, I don't care what we do or where we go, as long as we are in this boat, okay?"

"Okay, that I can do; how about we grab some hotdogs from Brud's and go out to watch the sunset?"

"That sounds like the best first date ever."

Later, at MacIntyre Lobster, the Finn family was hanging out having dinner. Jack had been smiling and acting funny. Russell had heard Jack had been running around in his boat with a girl on board. When Lucy and Anne got up to go to the bathroom, he took the moment to ask.

"So, who is the girl?"

"Girl... what girl?"

"The girl you had in your boat and ran out to Ram Island, then back to the Harbor with. Jack, your skiff is bright red, and you know every lobsterman on the water keeps an eye on you for me."

"Her name is Stephanie, Stephanie Turner. I am picking her up again tomorrow, and we are going to have some Brud's hotdogs and watch the sun set."

"That's ok, just remember, before it goes too far, she needs to come over for dinner with us."

"Why?"

"We are your parents, and we want to know who you are spending time with."

"What about Mom? You know how she can be."

"Yes, I do; her mother was the same way. Your mother brought you into this world; she has a right to meet anyone you are spending time with. It doesn't have to happen now, but soon."

"Ok, Dad."

CHAPTER SEVEN
Meadow

Jack looked at the truck; it wasn't perfect; it had some rust spots, but it started and had a new inspection sticker. He liked the old Chevy square bodies better, but Fords were not a bad truck. It was a 1997 Ford F-250 extended cab, four-wheel drive with a Fisher plow. It had faded emerald green paint and a red interior with vinyl seats that had some minor rips and tears.

"It's a 351 Winsza motah, fuel injected, nevah gave me any trouble." The old man had a thicker Maine accent than he and his father combined and was still talking to his father like he was the one buying it.

That was Jack's only issue with this truck. It was only eight years old; it was much newer than his father's old Chevy. Not only that, but his father's truck was a half-ton with a six-cylinder, while this truck was a three-quarter-ton with a V8 engine, and it had a plow. It didn't seem fair to him to have a better truck than his father.

"Sir, why are you selling it so cheap?" Jack asked.

"Wiscasset Ford had this thing on the lot for almost a year, and nobody would touch it. I guess people forgot how to drive standards. That, and she is kinda plain on the inside; you got to roll your own windows and such."

That wasn't what Jack wanted to hear; he wanted a reason to back out of the sale. He looked over at his dad's old Chevy and back at the truck before him. Russell saw this and read it for what it was. He knew how to handle this.

"Listen, Jack, you get this truck, and you will be plowing out the driveway every snowstorm free of charge, and you will be helping your mother with her trips to Conley's Greenhouse in the spring. Not to mention runs to Brooks Trap Mill; oh yeah, you get this pickup, and your chore list is going to get longer. You just keep that in mind with whatever else you are thinking over there."

He could always count on his dad to read his mind. He knew what his father had just said without actually saying it. That was the Russell Finn magic.

"Okay, sir, I will take it."

Jack gave the man the envelope with the money in it, and the man wrote up a bill of sale. While Jack and the old man were conducting business, Russell attached the transit plate issued by the town office.

"Alright, boy, how about you follow me home? Just be sure to keep your head up and eyes open; don't want you to run me over."

"Okay, Dad." Jack started his new truck; he had already test-driven it earlier, but now it was his. The old man had put the plow on to make it easier to sell. Jack hit the switch to clutch in the hydraulic pump, then lifted the plow up, then turned the hydraulics back off. He knew he would be looking a little foolish driving with a snowplow in late August, but he would be looking pretty smart come winter when he had a couple of driveways to plow and was making money. He stepped on the clutch and shifted the truck into first gear. He gently rested his foot on the gas pedal. He heard the engine rev slightly and slowly let off the clutch, and the truck moved forward, but something felt wrong. "Damn e-brake!" Jack reached down and released the emergency brake. He gave a wave out of the window to the old man who was counting the money in his envelope again.

The inside of the truck smelled musty and stagnant; he would have to do something about that before taking Stephanie for a ride. He turned on the radio and found it was on a country station, but it was playing that damn Jane Watson again. He changed the station to 102.9 WBLM. "It's a rock and roll kind of day, I think," he thought to himself. He rolled down his window to try to vacate the musty smell that seemed to be getting worse. There was no AC, just hot and cold air. It did have the little triangle windows that most old trucks had. He didn't dare reach across the cab to roll down the passenger window. He felt like a king in his "new to him" truck—no more school bus or riding with his sister Lucy and her cackling friends. He wouldn't have to ask his mother for the keys to take Stephanie on a date. He always took his mother's car because his father's truck reeked of vanilla pipe tobacco. He slowed down a little to get some room between him and his father, then stepped on the gas. The engine sounded good and healthy. He could see his father shaking his head from side to side.

He pulled into the driveway and off to the side to take the plow off with the help of his father. Then he pulled it into the middle of the dooryard and got out the hose and a bucket of water with some Dawn dish detergent. He then spent an hour and a half washing, waxing, and cleaning the interior of the truck. After he was done vacuuming, he put on the permanent plates. His mother had gone out and gotten him some pine-scented air fresheners; " smellies", she called them. He hung one from the rearview mirror. He sat down in a lawn chair to admire his truck.

"What you gonna do now, boy?" his father asked.

"I think I will give Stephanie a call and take her out for a ride."

"Sounds good; just remember we are hauling tomorrow; going to put in a long one to make up for what we missed today."

"Okay, Dad."

Jack ran into the house and dialed Stephanie's number. After three rings, he heard Stephanie's mother on the other end. "Hello."

"Mrs. Turner, this is Jack; is Stephanie there?"

"No, Jack, Stephanie took an extra shift at the Ice Cream Factory. She won't be out of work until nine o'clock."

"Oh, well... Mrs. Turner... may... I just got my new truck; would it be ok if I picked her up for you?"

"Jack, that would be fine with me, but she is staying with her father for a few days; you will have to call him."

"Okay, thank you, Mrs. Turner."

Jack was happy his parents were still together; Stephanie's parents had been divorced for as long as she could remember. Jack dialed the other number he had memorized.

"Hello, Robert Turner speaking."

"Hi, Mr. Turner, this is Jack. I heard Stephanie is working late tonight, and I was wondering if I could pick her up from work."

"Jack, Jack, Jack, how many times have I told you that you can call me Rob?

"Yes, sir...Rob."

"Did you get that truck you were looking at?"

"Yeah, I just cleaned it. I am anxious for Stephanie to see it."

"That's great. Hey, I got some family coming into town tomorrow; could I buy about   a dozen good-sized lobsters from you?"

"Yeah, a dozen, pound and a quarter, let's say fifty dollars?"

"That sounds like you are selling way under retail, but I won't argue."

"Okay, I will drop them off around five o'clock tomorrow; is that alright?"

"Sure. Hey, Jack."

"Yeah, Rob,"

"No funny business with my daughter."

"Yes, sir."

"Alright, Jack, see you later."

Jack took a breath after hanging up the phone. Since he and Stephanie had started being boyfriend and girlfriend, things had been getting serious. He hated to compare what they had to the juvenile base system that his friends used to brag about making it to home base with a girl. He and Stephanie had rounded first and were moving slowly to second. There had been no discussion by either party about going any further.

Jack was waiting outside of the Ice Cream Factory when Stephanie got out of work. He played the gentleman role and opened the door for her and helped her in. Her hair was being held back by a scrunchie, which she promptly removed and then shook out her hair. She placed the scrunchie over the shift lever and slid next to him .

"How do you like the truck?" asked Jack.

"I like it; it's big and green and clean." Stephanie said as she explored the interior with her eyes.

"Well, I gave her a good washing, inside and out, especially in here."

"Can we go to our spot, the one up on Spruce Point?"

"Sure."

While driving, Stephanie set the presets to the stereo, saving the number five spot for 94.9 WHOM, known for playing slow songs at night. She left it there and just enjoyed the music and the ride with Jack. Her head rested on his shoulder and her left hand on his lap. Jack did his best to shift gears without moving his right arm. Once they reached the top of Spruce Point, a spot Jack had found on his dirt bike years ago, they would sit on the tailgate and enjoy the view. It overlooked Linekin Bay, and with the moon full, the water sparkled below.

"Back to school in a few weeks. Sophomore year, not many sophomores have their license and a vehicle, Jack."

"I know; you sure have a good taste in boyfriends."

"I am nervous, Jack. We have had a great summer together, but it's just been the two of us. What happens when we go back to our friends and... everything?"

"Nothing is going to happen; if your parents let me, I will pick you up for school. Hopefully, our lunchtimes will be the same, and I can take you home."

"But what if I want to do cheerleading?"

"So do cheerleading; that will be cool! I will be dating a cheerleader!"

Stephanie slapped his leg playfully. "Jack, I am serious; aren't you worried about school messing us up?"

"Nope, not in the least."

"Why?"

"Because we have something special."

The answer was so simple and honest that Stephanie couldn't argue; not only could she not argue, but she also felt more sure about her and Jack. She decided she didn't need to talk about it anymore.

"I like your truck; are you going to name it?"

"I don't know; I haven't thought about it. Do you want to name it?"

She looked at the bed of the truck and remembered the green color as Jack pulled up to pick her up.

"Meadow, we will call her Meadow.

"Meadow...why Meadow?"

"Because it's big and green."

Jack turned now towards the bed of the truck. "You hear that, Meadow? You've got a name."

They laid back, Stephanie resting her head on his shoulder and Jack playing with her hair. They looked up at the stars and talked about the future.

CHAPTER EIGHT
Homecoming

STEPHANIE WAS WAITING AT HER father's kitchen table; he had already gone to work. She heard the distinct rumble of Meadow's engine, followed by the sound of Jack singing along with Toby Keith. She walked out the door and got in the truck. They had agreed that he would only open the door for her when out on dates.

"You ready for day one?" Jack asked.

"Yeah, I think so. I can't believe we still have three more years of high school; last year took forever," responded Stephanie.

"You still planning on cheerleading?"

"Yes, I have a meeting after school; my mother is coming to pick me up. Are you going to go haul after school?"

"No, I will haul on Saturday."

The small talk continued until they got to school. Mr. Farrin had a rule that shop class students could park outside his shop as long as they left their keys, they were not late, and they kept their grades up. Jack parked the truck just behind Mr. Farrin's old Dodge pickup.

"I am going to like not having homeroom this year; it will make the day go by faster. You have first lunch, right?" asked Stephanie.

"Yes, I have shop class, then English with Mr. Williamson, then lunch. Now for a possibly awkward question, do we sit together for lunch, or would you rather hang out with your friends?" answered Jack.

"Ahh, very good awkward question. Let's try sitting together; I mean, we have been seen together over the summer; I am sure after two periods the word will be out, and what is the big deal anyway?"

"Together it is. I will see you at lunch."

They kissed quickly and went into school via the shop door.

When lunch came around, Jack saw Stephanie sitting with one of her friends. The cafeteria had a serving line at the head of the room; along with the serving line, it had an à la carte line and a salad bar. The ladies that ran the lunchroom were those that he had seen out in the community but didn't always remember their names. Either way, they were always nice, so he returned the courtesy. Last year, Jack had asked his parents if he could just buy his own lunch from the à la carte and salad bar line. He made plenty of money, and he didn't always like what they had; Russell and Anne agreed to that.

The cafeteria had rectangular tables that seated six around the walls, then smaller round tables seating four in the middle. Seniors that had shop class could eat in the shop room that was across the hall; the same went for senior art students, who could eat in the art classroom. These rules were often bent a little if a senior had an underclassman friend. Jack grabbed a cheeseburger, tater tots, and carrot sticks and paid at the register. Stephanie was sitting next to the wall across from her friend. He sat in the middle seat next to Stephanie.

"Hey, babe," Stephanie said to Jack.

"Hi, how is your day going?" asked Jack.

"Good, this is my friend Sarah; she is a senior; we had art together last period. Sarah, this is my boyfriend, Jack."

"Hey Sarah, nice to meet you."

"So, how long have you two been together?" asked Sarah.

"Since, like, the last week of June." Stephanie replied.

Jack waved over one of his friends, who sat down on the corner opposite Jack. Then one of Sarah's friends sat down. Jack gave Stephanie a smile, and they sat and ate and got acquainted with their new friends.

Friday afternoon, Stephanie went home with Jack to hang out for a while. Jack's parents were home, and they all sat out on the porch, taking in the last of the warm weather.

"Can I go sternman with you tomorrow, Jack?" asked Stephanie.

"Sure, I don't mind the company, but I will have to pick you up early." replied Jack.

"Oh, crap, I forgot you were hauling your own gear tomorrow. I was hoping to get you to go with me." said Russell

Before Jack responded, Stephanie spoke up, "I will go with you, Russell! I have gone with Jack a few times."

Russell contemplated this for a moment. He had trawl strings to haul, which could be a struggle, but didn't want to sell Stephanie short.

"Go in the house and call to ask both of your parents; tell them we will be out for around six hours; if they have any other questions, come get me."

Stephanie ran into the house and was there for a while. She was all smiles when she came back out.

"It's a go!"

"Alright then, you have been over here for dinner enough times; Anne knows if you are allergic to anything; she makes up the snacks and lunches. I will come pick you up at five in the morning. You need to be up and ready to go. I will not beep the horn; if I pull in and see no lights on, I will back right back out of the driveway."

"I will be up; I am staying at my mother's house tonight."

"Ok then, you better get some sleep tonight and not stay up too late with this chowdah head," Russell said, gesturing at Jack.

The next morning Stephanie was up and ready to go; it was nice out, so she sat on the front porch until she heard the rattle and clatter of Russell Finn's truck. He had the windows open and put his pipe away while she was in the truck, but she could still smell the vanilla pipe tobacco; the interior had basically been marinating in it over the years. They pulled into the driveway at the Finns' house. They walked down the hill, onto the dock, and into the boat. Russell fired off the engine and untied the boat. Stephanie knew from going with Jack just what to do. Russell passed her a spare set of oilskins to put on. She had bagged herring before with Jack and started stuffing bags. After getting out on open water, Russell shut the engine off, stepped away from the helm, grabbed a big orange bumper, and tossed it overboard.

"Oops, I just fell overboard; you better go get me before I drown." Russell said.

Stephanie guessed that Russell didn't know Jack had shown her how to run this boat. There were a few days during the summer when it was raining, and Russell had let Jack borrow his boat. Stephanie had gone with him on some of those days, and she almost got lost in the memory of them dancing in the rain one afternoon. She went to the helm and started the engine, then put it in gear and idled to the bumper and grabbed it out of the water.

Russell stood in shock; it wasn't what he had expected. Stephanie looked at him, gave him a wink, and said, "Who do you think runs the boat while Jack cleans up?"

"Well then, I am in good hands. There is a spare knife on those oilskins. When you go with Jack, you normally fish singles, maybe a few secret pairs. We will be starting out the day hauling strings. If you step in the rope of a string, you will be pulled overboard. I will be watching you, but you need to know what to do, just in case. If you find yourself in the rope and being pulled over, keep your mind about you. Yell as loud as you can at me; don't fight the rope, you will lose; it will just pull tighter and make you panic. Stay calm and get your knife out and start cutting; if you have to go over the side, just do it".

Stephanie nodded; Jack had told her this before. Russell walked back to the helm and started cruising out of Linekin Bay. Russell was impressed with her knowledge of the islands; no doubt during the summer, Jack had taken her around all of them. He looked back to see her diligently filling bait bags.

He had liked Stephanie from the first time he met her. As a rule, both Jack and Lucy had to have anybody they were dating come over for dinner. This was a rule that Anne's father had, and Anne liked it, so she continued the tradition.

Russell still remembered walking into Anne's parents' house and her father's tight grip as he shook his hand and his steely stare. Stephanie handled it with grace and confidence, even with a hint of nostalgic class by putting a bow in her hair like the girls of the fifties.

Stephanie wasn't shy at all, not even around Anne's intimidating nature; he guessed Jack had already tipped her off about his mother actually being a loving and caring person. The same went for her interactions with Lucy, who, since Jack's birth, had always been a little protective of him. Lucy earned the nickname "little momma" for a while when they were growing up. Stephanie handled all the questions with confidence, but with a slight hesitation about anything involving her parents, so the Finns avoided that subject. At the end of the night, Jack was rewarded with an approving look from his mother.

Since then, it seemed Stephanie spent more and more time at their house; rather than going out on dates, they would often rent a movie and order pizza and go to Jack's room, door open. Stephanie had started coming over for the Finn Family Sunday breakfasts, which she enjoyed because Anne always had her and Lucy in the kitchen, teaching them how to cook, but it was so much more than cooking. It was mentoring, bonding, and sisterhood.

Now here she was out on the boat and looked like she was enjoying it. She was nowhere near as fast as Jack was, but nobody he took ever was. She was a hard worker and had a good attitude. She kept the pace up all day; they had a break while heading in from the islands, but they didn't have a chance to talk. At noon, Russell idled to the middle of Linekin Bay and shut down the engine.

"Finally, some peace and quiet," said Russell, digging out some sandwiches from his lunchbox. "Oh boy, meatloaf sandwiches! These are a treat, I tell ya! Anne puts leftover meatloaf and smashed tater in a big ole submarine roll. Not even Jack can eat more than one; this is the type of sandwich that will stick to your ribs!"

He passed a sandwich to Stephanie; she didn't know what to think at first about eating cold meatloaf and mashed potatoes, but after the first bite, the flavor was so good, she couldn't stop. There had been no wind that day, and as they ate their lunch, a gentle, warm breeze passed over them.

"My grandmother told me when a breeze comes like that, it's someone who loved you but died, checking in on you, sometimes answering you. She was part Native American, so she had a lot of beliefs like that." Stephanie said she didn't know why she said it; she just felt so comfortable with Russell.

"Makes sense to me, Steph, A breeze like that came through the cove not long after my father died. It's good to know someone is watching over us. It can be wicked dangerous out here. You are doing alright, though. How do you feel?"

"I know I will be hurting later, but this has been fun. I have always envied Jack's life out here on the water."

"Whenever you want some time on the water, you just let me know. I will take you along any day."

They finished their lunch and started hauling again. They were inside the bay now, so they were hauling pairs. The tempo was much slower with pairs, so Russell and Stephanie talked more now. They were bonding, and both of them knew it. Russell was like an uncle of sorts, full of wisdom and jokes and pointing out houses and different places along the water. She heard some conversations on the radio.

"Does Jack ever call you?" she asked.

"Not often; he is usually with me, but on days when he is on his own, he calls me to let me know when he is headed in. I try to check in with him, but he blasts his music so damn loud he can't hear the VHF. He had some stuff on the other day, and it just sounded like some guy screamin'. I asked what the heck it was, and he said, "Disturbed." I said, it sure is! Well, we got two more pairs, and we are done."

Stephanie was both relieved and slightly sad at the same time. She was tired but really enjoyed the time out here. They hauled the last two pairs and cleaned up the boat. Russell sat back at the transom while Stephanie ran the boat. While cruising, her eyes caught Jack coming up beside them in his skiff. His hat was turned backwards with his dirty blonde hair curling up around the edges. Russell walked up behind her.

"He can beat us, but do you want to race him anyway?"

"Sure, can I?"

"I don't know; can you?" With that, Russell made a nod to the throttle handle.

Stephanie pushed the throttle ahead a little, and Jack answered back. She crept the throttle more, and he sat down on his trap deck and throttled up more. She pushed the throttle until it wouldn't go any further. Jack gave a sinister grin, then hit the throttle all the way. The red skiff shot away like a scared cat.

"We go about twenty-six knots; Jack goes about thirty-five, but I have a roof over my head!"

That night, she and Jack decided to watch the newest Melissa Andrews movie, but she was so tired she fell asleep shortly after the movie started. Jack didn't bother to wake her; he just let her stay there asleep until the movie was over.

The routine at school had set in, and the weeks started to creep by. Boothbay Region High School was ramping up for Homecoming. Monday was career day; Jack had bought a fresh pair of oilskins so they wouldn't stink and went as a lobsterman. Stephanie, not really knowing what career path she wanted yet but knowing she was good with math and accounting, went as a banker. Tuesday was flannel day; Wednesday was camo or hunter orange day. Thursday was crazy outfit day, and then Friday was blue and gold day, the school colors. Jack volunteered to tow the sophomores' float with Meadow; Stephanie was on the cheerleaders' float. After the parade, the crowd collected around a big bonfire. Jack and Stephanie held hands while watching the fire.

Having each other seemed to make the school year go by faster, and they enjoyed having each other to share the moments. When winter came and school would be cancelled due to snow, Jack would pick up Stephanie while on his snowplowing route. He always had a mug of hot chocolate for her and a pumpkin donut from the Crunchy Snail bakery. She had also learned she could not sit right next to him when he was plowing; an accidental shift handle to the knee made that apparent. It still felt cozy in the cab of the truck, with the warm cocoa and the snowflakes falling around them.

When Christmas rolled around, they enjoyed Boothbay Harbor's many Christmas traditions together. It bothered her that her parents wouldn't get more involved; they seemed like hermits to her, both of them working or just watching TV at home. Not the Finns, though; they too were taking in the Boothbay Harbor Christmas scene. Stephanie felt so much a part of the family. The night of Christmas Eve, the Finns invited her and her parents over for dinner. Her parents made halfhearted excuses because they wouldn't come. Stephanie knew it was because her father couldn't bear to be in the same room as her mother. She didn't let that faze her, though; she had found the perfect gifts for Jack and Russell. Anne would like hers too, but Jack's and Russell's would be the best.

After dinner, they gathered in the living room for the gift exchange. Stephanie figured that Jack would give her a *Red at Night* hoodie, or a CD, or something practical. He came out of his room with a small box. She opened it up, and there was a small piece of dark blue sea glass that had JF+ST etched into it. It had a fine gold chain on it. Jack cleared his throat, then said, "That is from Ram Island, where we went the first day I met you. I picked it up that day to give to you but forgot it in my pocket."

"Jack, it's beautiful; thank you." She gave him a hug; they still didn't kiss in front of parents.

"We got you something too, dear; it was Russell's idea, but I think you will like it," said Anne as she passed her an envelope.

She opened the envelope to find a State of Maine recreational lobster license and a note telling her to look in the garage. She sprang up without saying a word and looked in the garage. There was a stack of five brand-new three-foot lobster traps. They were the "super threes" that Russell had that fished so well with the shrimp twine heads and a little wider than the normal three-foot traps. On top of the stack was a giant bow. She loved it and squealed with glee. She turned to Russell and gave him a hug and a kiss on the cheek. She turned and gave Anne a hug as well.

"Well, I never thought I would see the day where a sixteen-year-old girl would be excited about lobster traps," said Anne.

They went back to the living room. Stephanie reached into a bag and pulled out three items. They were flat, about an inch thick, and a little over a foot in length and width. She looked at the tags and passed them out. She asked Anne to open hers first. Anne tore open the wrapping paper to see a picture of herself with Lucy and Jack all sitting on the picnic table laughing. It was the type of picture you felt; you remembered that moment. Stephanie also knew that Anne's soft spot was her kids. She could see Anne had rolled a little of her bottom lip into her mouth and was biting it, obviously to steady herself. Anne then took a deep breath and said, "Thank you, dear."

"Ok, you two, go ahead; I want you to unwrap them at the same time," said Stephanie.

Both Jack and Russell tore into their gifts, finding watercolor paintings of their boats painted on a navigational chart of Lobster Cove. They lifted them up for the room to see, then each gave Stephanie a hug. Stephanie reached back in the bag and pulled out one more gift. She and Lucy had agreed that there was no need for a gift exchange between them, but when Stephanie was looking through pictures, she found a good one of Lucy and Jack sitting on the tailgate of Russell's truck together. She remembered how she had to try to sneak taking the picture. She knew just how much Lucy was protective of Jack and loved him so much—more than she ever told him. She and Lucy had bonded a little slower than the rest of the family. Stephanie passed the gift to Lucy, who immediately started to giggle.

"Great minds think alike, girl," said Lucy as she reached under the chair she was sitting in and pulled out a small present.

Lucy opened hers first and smiled wide. Then Stephanie opened hers from Lucy, and keeping up with the theme of pictures, she found a picture of her and Lucy standing on the dock together.

"I made the frame myself; I made it from some old trap runners, so it will smell like the ocean."

Stephanie held the frame to her nose, and Lucy was right. She gave Lucy a hug that lasted a while.

Later that evening, Stephanie lay in her bed, reflecting on the evening. She now had more than a boyfriend; she had an extended family of sorts. It terrified her and also made her feel warm. What would happen if they broke up? That question only lingered for a moment. The Finns were not the type to turn their back on someone. No matter what the future held for her and Jack, she knew she could always count on them.

While most students took advantage of snow days and slept in, not Jack, which also meant not Stephanie. Jack would listen to the weather the night before, then set his alarm for early morning. He would eagerly wait by the scanner, waiting to hear if school was canceled. Sure, you could wait for Joe Cupo on "Storm Center" to tell you, but if you wanted to be the first to know, you had a scanner, and you listened for either Helen Hitt, Barbara Lorraine, Hilda Lewis, Barbara Fossett, Mary Lewis, or one of the many other dispatchers that were in the Boothbay Harbor Town Office to announce it.

Jack would pick Stephanie up as early as her parents would allow, always with hot cocoa and a pumpkin donut from the Crunchy Snail. Meadow was always warm and toasty, so much so that they would keep the little triangle windows open for fresh air. Watching Jack plow was entertaining in itself; she often wondered how it was possible that he could do so much and be so coordinated.

The constant shifting, which involved one hand and then also a foot on the clutch, and then there was operating the plow with his left hand, so he would have to take his hand off the shift lever and put that on the steering wheel. When he got to the end of a driveway, he would have to push the clutch in with his left foot and hit the brake with his right foot, shift into reverse with his right hand, and then lift the plow with his left. It didn't always go so smoothly; he stalled the engine several times in several driveways when he first started, but in the typical Finn fashion, Jack didn't give up. If anything, it fueled him to get it right.

Along with watching Jack shuffle the many controls, there was also the fun of just being in the truck while plowing: the sound of the engine revving to push the snow, the plow grading across the frozen drive, and then the sudden jerk of the truck coming to a stop if Jack didn't hit the brake fast enough. All this was combined with constant conversation and the radio in the background.

Just like out on the water, the plow guys all seemed to look out for each other; that may have had something to do with many of the plow guys being lobstermen. And of course, they always had an eye out for Jack and went the extra mile to help him out. Stephanie had observed during the summer, and now in the winter, that when these guys saw a young person like Jack working hard, they didn't just respect it; they wanted to help and even be a part of it. In the summer, Jack hardly ever had to pay for bait because the guys always would leave some in the bait room labeled "for the kids." The gill netters would bring in skates and sculpins to add to the stash. Now in the winter, these guys wouldn't hesitate to give Jack a hand if he got his truck stuck or had an issue with the plow. One guy helped Jack change out a hydraulic hose and gave him some hydraulic fluid. Stephanie would do her part and help shovel out the walkways and porches.

Winter slowly passed, and spring began to bloom. Over the winter, Stephanie had taken and passed her driver's education class and now had her permit. The law was clear that she couldn't drive with just Jack in the vehicle, but that didn't stop Jack from teaching Stephanie how to drive a standard. At first, they started in the YMCA parking lot at night, and then after she got the hang of it, Jack would let her drive on some of the older back roads or around Barter's Island. Jack's truck was huge compared to her parents' cars. It looked and felt like the truck took up the entire road.

One Saturday afternoon, she had her mother drop her off at the Finns' house. Anne was outside getting ahead in the spring gardening.

"Hello, Anne. Is Jack in yet? He said they would be in by three," asked Stephanie.

"I went down and called on the radio not too long ago. Russell wants to take advantage of the tides and take another load out. I told Jack I would take you with me to Conley's so you wouldn't have to wait here by yourself; that is, if you want to come," Anne replied.

"Yes, I would be glad to."

"Alright then, hop into Russell's truck."

Anne and Stephanie hopped into the truck. When Anne tried to start it, the engine rolled once, then twice, and then the starter made a clicking sound.

"Goddamn this old truck, why doesn't he just get rid of it?" Anne paused, then turned to Stephanie. "I am sorry about that. I just have been anxious to get going on the garden, and I can't fit anything in my car."

"Can't we just take Jack's truck? I am sure he wouldn't mind."

"Stephanie... I can cook, I can plant, I can sew, I can shuck scallops, pick shrimp, and fillet a fish. I can even hold my own on a lobster boat. I am a strong Maine woman to my bones. The one thing I can't do is drive standard."

If not for such a moment, Stephanie would have laughed. Anne was so strong; she projected such strength like an aura around her. But, here, Stephanie could do something Anne couldn't.

"Anne, I can drive Jack's truck; he taught me."

"We need to go to Conley's, dear, not quite as simple as driving around in the school parking lot."

"Anne, don't get mad, but I have driven on Butler Road, some other dirt roads, and around Barter's Island."

Anne had a mixed bag of feelings, but in the end, the conversation she wanted to have with Stephanie and the sale on spring flowers won.

"Okay, let's go."

Stephanie was nervous; not only was this her first time one-on-one with Anne, but now she was driving Meadow, big giant Meadow. She could see Anne had a tight grip on the door handle, so she went slow and easy, easing off the clutch so the truck wouldn't lurch forward.

Anne noticed the confidence Stephanie had; she had driven this truck and driven it well. She could shift gears without a hitch. She instructed Stephanie to take the long way to Conley's rather than going over Horse Hill. Once she saw Barret's Park parking lot, she asked Stephanie to pull in and park.

"STEPHANIE, I AIN'T GOING TO sugarcoat this; this is going to be an awkward conversation, but I believe we need to have it." She paused to take a deep breath and exhaled slowly; she had thought about this conversation and rehearsed it in her head several times. She had even thought about calling Stephanie's mother, but she just wasn't sure about that. How would she even start that conversation? It wasn't the fact that they could be having sex that bothered her, though she hoped they weren't; it was their future she was worried about, and not just her son's. If Stephanie got pregnant, it would change their lives forever. Anne took another deep breath and started to speak. But Stephanie beat her to it.

"Jack and I aren't having sex yet," blurted out Stephanie.

"Ah, ok, um, well, I had this all rehearsed, and now I don't know what to say."

"We have talked about it; that's it, and it's not going to be happening soon... oh, ok, and we know... um, condoms."

Anne could see Stephanie's face was bright red, and her knuckles were white from the grip on the steering wheel. "Ok then... that's all I need to know, just... um, if you need to talk... you know."

Stephanie pulled out of the parking lot, not knowing what to say or if she should tell Jack that it happened. Her parents had done the same and asked "how serious" it was getting. She didn't know what to think of Anne asking her. Had Russell talked to Jack about it? She had told Jack that she wanted to wait until she was older, and Jack had no issues with it. She sat there, hoping Anne would say something to break the awkward silence.

"Did you hear that Melissa Andrews got emancipated from her mother? I guess her mother is a tyrant. I can't imagine having a daughter so talented and not wanting to be involved." Anne said, trying to change the subject.

"Yeah, Jack said you were a big fan of hers." Stephanie replied, so glad that the awkward moment was over.

"Yes, I am. She reminds me of the actresses back when I was her age."

"I think Jack's a fan too, but he doesn't say anything. I think he thinks I will be jealous."

"Oh, you know you don't have anything to worry about; my boy is quite taken with you."

"I am quite taken with him too, Anne; I am probably too young to say this, but you raised a good boy."

"Well, I thank you. You are quite the catch yourself; don't forget."

CHAPTER NINE
Young Love—The Judds

Jack and Stephanie had arrived at a party; it was being hosted by another member of the junior class. Her parents were out of town, and today was the last day of their junior year. They had been to a few parties before, but this one seemed to be much bigger. There were students swimming in the pool and soaking in a hot tub. The weeks leading up to this party had been a little tense between Jack and Stephanie. Stephanie was thinking about college, while Jack already knew what he was going to do. The thought of Stephanie moving away had made Jack possessive, trying to monopolize Stephanie's time. Even tonight, Jack wanted to spend time with Stephanie alone.

There was a keg of beer out on the porch along with various other alcohols on a table. Jack decided the best way to deal with this tension was to have a beer. He walked away from Stephanie, who was too busy talking to her friends anyway. He poured himself a beer, then another, and then he tried some whiskey. He looked back in the house and saw a boy dancing with Stephanie. He walked back into the house.

"What the hell is going on here?" Jack said, not so much a yell, but loud enough to get everyone's attention.

"Jack, he is just a friend; we were not even touching." Stephanie replied.

"Yeah, for now; how long before you sneak off together?"

"Jack, have you been drinking? I think you need to slow down and cool off."

"Don't tell me to slow down and cool off while you are in here, turning up the heat."

"Jack... fuck off!" The minute she said it, she regretted it, but she was too proud to take it back in front of all her friends, and there was a part of her that thought he deserved it.

Jack thought of things to say back but instead turned around and went back outside. He grabbed the bottle of whiskey he had earlier and sat down in a chair and started drinking from the bottle. He looked over at the hot tub; there were just some girls in it now.

"That'll show her," he grumbled. He took off his shirt, but his fingers couldn't operate his belt buckle. He made a controlled stumble into the hot tub but maintained a grip on the whiskey bottle.

"Hello, ladies," he said as they laughed and giggled. He had never seen these girls before; they must have been freshmen or were going to be freshmen. He continued to drink while talking to the girls. When the bottle was gone, he decided to get out of the hot tub and get another. He found another partial bottle of something. He took a swig and continued to walk, shirtless, off the porch and down the driveway.

Stephanie had had enough of the looming tension. She had been talking to friends, but the verbal scuffle with Jack kept nagging at her. She went outside to find him but instead found his shirt, shoes, and socks on the deck. There was a trail of wet footsteps leading off the porch; she followed them down the driveway and onto the road, but they faded. She went back to the party and asked the girls in the hot tub about Jack. They referred to Jack as the hot senior, and they hadn't seen him since he went to get another bottle, gesturing at the bottle he left behind.

Jack was drunk and missing; it was dark out, and he was not wearing a shirt or shoes; this was bad. Her mind started reeling, thinking about every bad thing that could happen. At first, she didn't know what to do; should she try to go look for him? No, she was only one person and not in the best state of mind. "Russell," she said out loud—not really something she wanted to do, but it was the best move. She went inside and grabbed the phone and dialed the number she knew by heart.

"Hello?" She heard Russell's voice, somewhat startled and alert.

"Russell, this is Stephanie; I have lost Jack."

"Lost him... how? Is he ok?"

"I don't know; he is drunk; he doesn't have a shirt or shoes. We are at a party; it's on Lakeside Drive just before you get to West Harbor Pond."

Russell could hear the genuine fear and concern in Stephanie's voice; it was shaky and panicked.

"Ok, Stephanie, I will get there as soon as possible."

Anne was up as well and standing beside him.

"They went to a party; Jack got drunk and wandered off. I will call the police chief personally and let him handle that end on his own. I am going to pick up Stephanie and look for Jack. You stay here and stay by the phone."

Russell called the police chief on his personal line and let him know what was going on. The chief said he would send whoever was on shift to the area. Russell got in his truck and headed to the house.

As Russell drove, he contemplated the circumstances. Would Jack be, okay? It was warm out so he wouldn't freeze to death, but they were close to West Harbor Pond; he could fall in and drown; he could get hit by a car. He tried to change his thoughts; he tried to be more positive. Soon, he saw Stephanie outside at the end of the driveway; the party had dispersed. Stephanie got into the truck and then pointed in the direction where she thought Jack had gone. Russell passed her a handkerchief to clear her nose and dry her eyes. They hadn't gone far when they were passed by an ambulance with lights and sirens going. Russell sped up and chased after the ambulance, and the truck got eerily silent. As they followed the ambulance, they saw flashing blue lights ahead; it was a police car facing them, with Jack lying in the road. The police officer had him rolled over on his side while he vomited. The ambulance came to a stop, and Russell pulled over as well. The EMTs got out and hustled over to Jack, covering him with a blanket.

"He will be ok, Russell; he just drank too much. I think he should go to the hospital, though, just to be sure," said Officer Nick Upham.

"Yeah, I will go pick up Anne, and we will meet him at St. Andrews. He is okay, though?"

The EMT, Chris Mitchell, had finished taking vital signs and looked back at Russell. "He has minor alcohol poisoning; his heart rate is slow, as is his breathing. I will get him warmed up and put on an IV to get him hydrated. He will be fine, other than having one hell of a hangover."

Russell looked on as they loaded him into the ambulance. Stephanie was at his shoulder; she had stopped crying but was still sobbing.

"Russell, it's my fault; I got mad at him and swore at him," she said before Russell interrupted.

"Nope, this is Jack's fault; we have talked about alcohol and drinking before and talked about the risks. He let his anger cloud his judgment. Don't you blame yourself for this. Now I got to go home and get Anne. How about you call your parents from our house and let them know you are safe? If they want you to go home, we will drop you off, or you can come to the hospital with us."

They got in the truck and went to pick up Anne. Stephanie called her mother and let her know what was going on.

"Mom," Stephanie said into the phone when she heard her mother pick up.

"Stephanie, what in the world is going on? You were supposed to be home hours ago."

"Mom, Jack got really drunk and wandered off. I had to call Russell. We found Jack, but he is in the hospital; can I go with the Finns to see him? They will bring me home after."

"Stephanie... have you been drinking?"

"Yes, Mom, I had a couple of beers."

"We will talk when you get home; go ahead and check on Jack."

They went to the hospital and went to Jack's room. He was sleeping and had an IV going into his arm. They stood there looking at him for only a moment before he opened his eyes.

Jack looked up at his mother, father, and Stephanie and was overwhelmed with guilt. The look of worry still hung on all their faces. Stephanie's makeup had run down her cheeks; his mother had puffy eyes, so he knew she had cried or was about to. His father had a look of relief and disappointment. Jack couldn't help but start to cry himself; he started sobbing, "I'm sorry, I'm so sorry."

The Finns gave Stephanie a ride home after the visit. She slept in late the next morning, physically and emotionally exhausted. She was thankful this happened on a night she stayed with her mother; her father would not have been so easy. In the afternoon, she drove to the Finns' house and knocked on the door. Jack answered, looking better than he did in the hospital, but not great.

"Hi," he said in a low voice.

"Jack, let's go down to the dock and talk."

He tossed on his shoes and followed her down to the dock. As they walked down, neither said a word. Jack was thinking that Stephanie would yell at him a little for scaring her, but that would be it. He had messed up, but they had been through a lot. He just needed to apologize first, before she started, and that would help diffuse the situation. When he got down the ramp and was standing on the float, he started to speak, but Stephanie cut him off.

"Wait, Jack, I have things to say. I do owe you an apology for telling you to 'fuck off' last night; not that it is an excuse, but you had been pushing me to it for the month. I am not your property; I can hang out with whoever I want to, whenever I want to. I need space, Jack. I need to be able to breathe."

"What are you saying?"

"Jack, I think we need to go our separate ways. Seeing you get so jealous and controlling at just the mere thought of me going away for college has made me change the way I look at you. You almost died because you couldn't even handle it yourself." Stephanie was crying now, but her words sounded so harsh.

"So that is it; we are done, just like that. All the times in my boat, all the times in Meadow. The night we..."

"Stop it, Jack; just stop. All that will always mean something, but we need to move on. I need to move on." She wanted to hug him, but it just wasn't there. She started walking up the hill, wondering if this was the right move, but Jack had been very controlling the past month, trying to monopolize her time. At the top of the hill, in the Finns' driveway, as she turned to get into her car, she looked down at the dock to see Jack staring back at her; she considered waving or maybe running back down the hill. Her eyes started to well up more; she opened the car door, got in, and left the Finns' driveway.

Jack stayed in his room for the rest of the weekend. At first, he was sad, just watching his TV but not really engaged in what was on. Then he got angry and took everything Stephanie had ever given him and stuffed it in a box, along with all the pictures he had of her. He was going to throw it all away but decided to put it in the back of his closet, way back where he wouldn't see it. Monday morning came, and Russell was about to knock on his door when he heard Jack's alarm go off. He listened in at the door and heard he was getting ready. Soon, both were walking down to the boat; Jack wasn't saying anything, just going through the motions. Russell untied the boat and headed out of Lobster Cove.

Once out of the cove and in more open water, Russell shut the boat off.

"Alright, Jack, time to start talking."

"About what?"

"Jack, I already know you are too smart to ask such a dumb question. I want to know what happened Friday night, and I want to know what happened between you and Stephanie."

Jack took a long, deep breath and pressed it out between his lips like he was blowing out a candle. He sat down on the washrail of the boat and looked up at his father.

"At the party, I saw her dancing with another guy, and with her looking at schools out of state, it just made me feel like I was losing her. So, I decided to drink and figured if I was drunk, I wouldn't care. Next thing I know, Officer Upham is standing over me, and I am lying in the road. Then I am waking up and seeing all your faces. Then the next day Stephanie comes over and dumps me. I messed up, Dad. I messed up big time."

"Yeah, you did. I have half a mind to take away your truck and boat for a while, but something tells me you learned your lesson. Son, you scared the shit out of me, your mother, and Stephanie. Lucy would have been scared too if she hadn't been asleep."

Russell paused for a moment to think about what to say next. He took a long pull from his pipe and exhaled, letting the smoke circle around his head.

"Jack, there is nothing I can tell you that will fix the hurt you are feeling about Stephanie. To tell you the truth,

I am disappointed in you for how you have been treating her recently. I saw you trying to control her, and now I feel like I probably should have said something sooner. She is a bright young woman with a mountain of potential, and you want her to waste that because you two may break up! Where did that get you? Jack, you should have been supporting her, pushing her up. If your love for each other was genuine, nothing could kill it, and even if you two went your separate ways, you could look back at it fondly."

Jack was struck by this; he figured his father would be on his side. His father was right, though; he had nobody to blame but himself.

"What do I do, Dad?"

"You need to give her space; first, she is hurt; she saw an ugly side of you; she needs time to process that. Then, when she is ready, you need to help her, even if it means just being her friend. Help her decide on what school to go to. Help her plan her room and board. Offer to help move her if you can. Jack, if you two had what I think you had, you will get her back. If not, it wasn't meant to be, but at least she will be in your life. Now, get your ass in gear; we got traps to haul."

Jack's mood improved as the day went on. Working out on the water, especially with his dad, had always been a sort of therapy for him. If his father ever needed another profession, he could be a psychiatrist. Jack knew he couldn't just jump in his truck and drive to Stephanie's and pour his heart out and get her back; nope, he needed to do just as his father said.

He waited a couple of days, then called her. He apologized and asked if she needed help with picking a school. He told her he wanted to at least stay friends. She agreed to that and felt the same. There were no more dates, though, no more kisses, and when they hugged, it felt odd and awkward.

Stephanie had started an accounting job at the beginning of the summer, working with a firm in town. She was a receptionist, but they started teaching her other parts of the business. She had a gift for numbers, and she liked the work. When not at the office, she would fill in as a sternman for a lobsterman, always double-checking with Russell first. It was her way to get out on the water; the more she went, the more she realized that it wasn't just the ocean she missed. Jack had seen her at the dock a couple of times, and it tugged at his heartstrings every time she said hi. He didn't dare ask if she was seeing anyone else. He did ask if she had picked a school yet; she said she was still weighing out her options.

Jack had finished hauling his own traps and pulled into MacIntyre Lobster to sell; he wanted to hurry because it looked like a storm was coming. When he went up to the office to get paid for the week, he noticed Stephanie there waiting.

"Waiting for your mom or dad?" asked Jack

"Yeah, Dad was supposed to pick me up, but he is stuck in a meeting; Mom is out of town. I don't like the way Dale Rines keeps looking at me. I am about to take my chances and walk home," replied Stephanie.

"Come with me; we can run to my house, then I can take you home in Meadow."

"What if it starts raining?"

"I have a spare raincoat in the boat that you can use, but I think I can outrun the storm in the *Red at Night*."

"Ok," they walked down the ramp together and stepped into the boat. Stephanie sat at the end of the trap deck to give Jack plenty of room. He was standing, his hat facing forward, as they idled out through the inner harbor. Jack saw the sky darken a little more.

"Hold on, Steph," he said as he took off his hat and turned it backwards. This whole time Stephanie had a feeling, like a beacon going off in her chest. She hadn't felt this way in a while. She gripped the trap deck tightly while Jack opened the throttle up on the outboard. *Red at Night* started skimming across the water. Suddenly the sky grew darker and more ominous, and the clouds started swirling in a devilish manner.

"Shit!" Jack said out loud. "Steph, open that tote under the trap deck. There is a raincoat in there. Put it on."

She opened the tote and found one raincoat; she looked for another; she knew he said he had a spare.

"Jack, I can only find one."

"I only have one."

"You said you had a spare."

If Jack wasn't so concerned with the upcoming weather, he might have felt more emotion about what he was going to say next; instead, it came out robotic.

"I lied to get you to come with me. Hold on a second; I need to call my dad."

Jack slowed down a little and turned towards the shore; he grabbed the microphone to his VHF radio. "Please be in the dock house, Dad, please be in the dock house," he said, before holding the microphone to his mouth and keying it in. "*Wicked*, you in the dock house?"

"Yeah, go ahead, Jack."

"Dad, I think a squall is coming on; I am going to hide under the dock just to the east of where we sold those lobsters yesterday. Can you run out here and get Stephanie? She is with me."

"Yup, I will be headed right out; remember to turn all your electronics off if it starts lightnin'."

"Got ya, Dad."

As if the sky heard the word and took it as a command, there was a loud crack, and a lightning bolt could be seen in the distance, followed by a clap of thunder that you could hear and feel. Raindrops the size of golf balls started coming down just as Jack snuck the boat in under a ramp. The rain was so fierce it drowned out all sound, and all you could hear was the rain hitting the dock and the water; it made an intense and loud hum. The ramp gave a little shelter, but water still leaked through the gaps in the boards.

"Listen, the wind is going to pick up pretty badly soon. I mean, really bad; it's going to be a little scary. You are safe, and when my dad gets here, you will be safer. It's just a microburst; it will only last five minutes or so, but it will be the longest five minutes of your life," said Jack, almost yelling to get his voice over the sound of the rain.

The wind started to pick up slowly at first, then it was howling. The dock made a huge cracking sound. Jack looked up to see the ramp was breaking away from the dock. He fired up the outboard and motored out from under the dock.

"Steph!" He had to yell now to make his voice heard over the wind that was now raging. "Put on that life jacket. Now!"

Stephanie heard the urgency; Jack had never ordered her to do anything before.

"Hold on tight; it's going to get sketchy."

"Going to get sketchy?" was all Stephanie could think; it was already sketchy in her book.

Jack could see his father heading his way. He poured on as much throttle as he could with the three-foot whitecaps. Because of the rain, there was three inches of water in his boat, and both bilge pumps were running. He needed to get Stephanie off the boat and safe, then he could either run into shore and beach the boat or make a run for home.

Both boats were bouncing heavily on the wave tops. Both Jack and his father knew they had to swap Stephanie over quickly.

"Steph, get up here on the trap deck; squat down so you are on one knee. My dad will grab you and pull you on board." Stephanie listened and did just what he said. She could see Jack was completely soaked; he looked like he had just jumped in the ocean. Jack had his left arm on the outboard tiller, and the other was holding her bicep; his grip was so tight she thought she might lose circulation in that arm. Despite how much the little skiff was being tossed around, Jack was as steady as an oak tree.

Russell had an idea of what Jack was thinking; he reached out and removed the snatch block from the davit so Stephanie wouldn't hit her head on it. They would time it so the skiff would be on an upward bounce, then Russell could grab her. Though his thirty-foot South Shore was being bounced around, he could leave the helm long enough to grab Stephanie. He looked to see Jack giving him a quick nod; it was go time. Jack swung the *Red at Night* in at an arc, with the peak of the arc being the middle of the side of Russell's boat. Russell did his best at the helm, holding *Wicked* steady. Jack was closing in; he left the helm, walked a few short steps, and grabbed Stephanie with both arms as if giving her a bear hug. It wasn't until Russell had both arms around her that Jack let go of her bicep. Russell looked at Jack and yelled, "Where is your life jacket?" Jack just pointed to Stephanie.

"Dad, I will try to follow you home and use your wake to knock down some of this slop; I may have to run to shore, though, and put this thing up on the ground; hopefully I can find a soft spot."

"I will runnah so she is draggin' the ocean; that should knock it down for ya."

Russell turned to Stephanie and said, "Sit down on the engine box and hold on."

Russell pushed the throttle up until *Wicked* had a bow-high altitude and was making the largest wake possible. Jack ran the *Red at Night* just behind the first wave from the stern, riding it to beat down the oncoming waves. Jack looked down to see he was only standing in an inch of water now. When his father looked back, he pointed to the bottom of his boat and then gave a thumbs-up.

The wind died down just as they got to Lobster Cove; they slowed down and idled up into the cove. Stephanie helped Russell tie his boat up while Jack was already tied up and was sorting through the stuff in his boat that had either gotten wet or knocked loose while being bounced around. Russell walked up the ramp whistling an old country melody. Stephanie took off the life jacket and the raincoat, despite it still raining slightly.

"What the hell is wrong with you, Jack Finn? Lying to me about the raincoat is one thing; giving me the only life jacket you had is another. Why did you do that?" she yelled while throwing the life jacket and raincoat at him.

"Just in case we lost you overboard trying to switch boats." Jack replied while catching the thrown objects and tossing them into his boat.

"But what about you, out there bouncing around in that skiff? What if you fell over? What if it sank?"

"Stephanie, nothing happened. I am fine; I am right here."

"That isn't good enough, Jack; I want to know why. I could tell you were scared. Why give me the raincoat and life jacket?"

"I wasn't scared," said Jack as he stepped out of his boat and tried to walk around Stephanie.

Stephanie stepped to the side, blocking his escape, and brought them so close that she could feel the warmth of his breath on her face. She was getting wet now too. Raindrops were running down both of their faces as the sun started making its effort to come out.

"You were scared, Jack Finn; don't tell me you weren't. I could hear it, I could see it, and I could feel it." Stephanie's voice gained pitch and volume with the cadence of the sentence.

"Yes, ok, I was scared. I was scared of losing you. Just like I was scared the night of the party, just like since you started looking at schools. I don't want to lose you. I guess the joke's on me, though; I lost you anyway. Sure, we are friends, but soon you will go off to college, meet some guy, and you will get married. Are you going to invite me to your wedding? At least that way, I know you are alive, well, and happy. I couldn't lose you to the ocean, not for good. I love you too much for that," said Jack, knowing what he was saying wasn't making sense; he was just talking from the heart now.

She wrapped her arms around him and kissed him passionately; at first, she could tell he was caught off guard, but he then held her and kissed her back.

Russell peeked out the window and sang quietly to himself the last two lines of the song he was whistling earlier.

"She was sitting cross-legged on the hood of a Ford, filing down her nails with an emery board."

CHAPTER TEN
Growing Up

IT HAD GONE BY SO fast; he remembered his parents and Lucy standing with him just outside the doors of the Boothbay Region Elementary School; now here he was in a blue gown, about to walk across the stage to get his diploma. He could see his parents and his big sister, Lucy, sitting in the typical uncomfortable folding chairs. They seemed to glow with pride as they anticipated hearing his name as much as he did. They were calling names in the order they were seated, not in alphabetical order. Stephanie had already gotten hers, and his parents cheered just as much as her parents did. Stephanie had become a fixture at his house, coming over for dinners and the famous Finn Family breakfast every Sunday morning. As Stephanie's parents had been divorced since she could remember, she was drawn to the family atmosphere. The person beside him had just been called; it was almost time; then, his name.

As Jack walked across the stage, memories of the past twelve years played in his head, sitting in the big concrete circle just outside the elementary school doors while his mother took a picture. All the report cards, the school concerts, the friends he had made over the years, and Stephanie. He remembered thinking that school was going to take forever; now it seemed so short. He grabbed the diploma with his left hand and shook the principal's hand with his right. He smiled at the camera, then walked around the big loop, back to his spot. After a few more names were called, they had the class stand up and receive a final round of applause from the crowd.

THE NEXT AND FINAL TRADITION was called "The Gauntlet." No one knew when it had started, but it was the final stop before students left the school for the last time. Having received their diplomas, they were no longer considered students anymore and were open to saying whatever they wanted to say to the teachers. Likewise for the teachers, as these were no longer their students, and they could say what they wanted to the former students.

There had been some colorful exchanges in the past, but more recently it was peaceful. Both teachers and students used it as a chance to offer final parting words, advice, and thanks. Even a few teachers from the elementary school would come over and participate. Jack made his way through the line, shaking hands and saying thank you to the teachers. Mr. Farrin said he would see him on the water. At the end of the line of teachers were the doors, and walking through them this time was the capstone.

They were now released to their families. Jack found Stephanie, and they walked out the door hand in hand. As soon as they were outside, they embraced in a big hug followed by a kiss.

"We did it, Jack!" announced Stephanie triumphantly.

"We sure did! Hard to believe, I mean, I think I am already going to miss this place, but on the other hand, I am so glad it is over."

"Well, it may be over for you; this girl will be going to the University of Southern Maine in Portland!" said Stephanie's father as he walked up.

Jack wasn't sure if that was meant to be a slight or if he was just proud. He decided not to take it personally. "Yeah, she will be one of the best accountants in Boothbay Harbor! She has been helping me keep my books for lobstering and plowing for years."

"Oh, Jack, you can't keep her locked up in Boothbay Harbor; Steph was made for bigger and better places."

All the joy had been sucked out of Jack; what was Rob trying to say?

"Dad, we talked about this. Don't ruin this moment." Stephanie interjected, fighting emotions.

Rob looked hard at Jack, then back at Stephanie. He saw the Finn family coming. "You are right, Steph; I will leave it alone. I will see you at the house later."

Before Jack could ask what that was all about, his family had arrived, with Stephanie's mother not far behind. Stephanie always felt so warm around the Finn family. They could always make her feel better, no matter the tensions in her life with her parents. After more hugs and more photos, it was time to get home for the graduation party. The Finns had offered to host both Jack and Stephanie's graduation party; they had a great location. Anne loved to host, and Stephanie's parents couldn't agree about which house to hold hers. Jack and Stephanie greeted people as they arrived and thanked people for their gifts. They visited with family members that had traveled to get there. As people started filtering out, Jack couldn't find Stephanie. He looked down at the dock and saw her sitting on the trap deck of his boat. He walked down to see her.

"Hey Stephanie, people are leaving. Are you ok?"

"Jack, he couldn't even come. He has such a hatred for my mother and this community that he wouldn't even come to this party. I had aunts and uncles here. I had to answer for him. What is he going to do if we get married?"

"Hold your horses now; we just graduated; we got some time to get things sorted out. Anyway, who says I am going to marry you? I may marry my side chick instead."

Stephanie belted out a laugh. "Jack Finn, with a side chick! Never in a million years! Not only are you too good of a man, but your family would also kill you if they ever found out."

Jack sat in the boat next to her. "Today is the first big milestone as we move forward. And who knows, this could be our last; things happen. Let's not worry about them; let's just live right now, and when tomorrow comes, we will face it together, then the next, then the next. If your dad doesn't want to be a part of that journey, we can't help it, but we can always leave the door open for him."

Stephanie kissed him softly and smiled.

"Time to get ready for the Grand March, then it's officially over," said Jack.

"No, Jack. It will be the beginning."

Boothbay Region High School held one of the country's oldest traditions, the Grand March, the evening after graduation. The school has kept this tradition for over one hundred years and is one of the few schools to still do it. The students are paired up, one boy and one girl. They march into the gymnasium four abreast before breaking off and moving about the gym in an elegant, choreographed march, separating down to two single-file lines and weaving in and out of each other. It's an extravagant sight to behold. At the end of the march, the boy dances with the girl's mother as the girl dances with the boy's father. After those dances, the event turns into a typical dance. Anne and Russell looked on as Jack danced with Stephanie.

The DJ announced that he was about to play the last song. Knowing that this would probably be the last moment these kids would spend together as a class, he decided not to choose some sappy love song; he wanted the kids, now green adults, to remember their childhood. So, he picked a song from a movie they would all know from years ago, and that would touch them.

Jack was already dancing with Stephanie; they stood facing each other, ready to hold each other and sway to the rhythm of some love song. Then they heard the first few lyrics.

> *You've got a friend in me*

> *You've got a friend in me*

"It's *Toy Story*!" Stephanie observed. She looked around at the rest of their classmates, all confused, looking at each other, but as the lyrics went on,

> *When the road looks rough ahead*

> *And you're miles and miles*

> *From your nice, warm bed*

> *You just remember what your old pal said*

> *Boy, you've got a friend in me*

> *Yeah, you've got a friend in me*

Each member of the graduating class joined hands, swaying to the rhythm and joining in singing every verse until the end. They received a large round of applause from the rest of the onlookers; there were very few dry eyes in the crowd.

"You ready to go?" asked Stephanie

To Jack, this question wasn't just about leaving the dance. This question really meant, was he ready to leave childhood behind, leave school behind, and start a new chapter in the book of Stephanie and Jack? The summer would be theirs as it had been for the past three years, but the next time he went out to haul his traps, he would no longer be a student, a kid; he would be doing it for real. His father had already told him he would be paying rent to stay in the house after school got out. Jack thought that was fair. Stephanie would work at Midcoast Payroll and Accounting this summer, but in the fall, she would be going back and forth to Portland to go to college. This really would be their last moment as kids.

"Yeah, I am ready to go; I will meet you down at Meadow; I want to change out of this tux."

"Me too; I am going to the locker room and change."

Later that night, while lying in the back of Jack's truck, Jack had to ask Stephanie about what her father was talking about.

"What did your dad mean about keeping you locked up in Boothbay Harbor, and you were meant for bigger and better places?

Stephanie sighed but knew she owed Jack an explanation.

"Jack.... I got accepted into other schools, one of them being Syracuse; that's where my dad wanted me to go, because that is where he is going. He took a job in New York. It was a part of a deal he and my mom made when they got divorced; they would stay in the same location until I graduated. A firm in New York offered him a position, and he figured I would go to school there."

"But you couldn't leave your mother," said Jack.

"No, I couldn't leave you. Jack, I don't want to rush us, but I feel we are meant to be together, to spend the rest of our lives together. My dad read me like a book; he knew I wanted to stay because of you. That's when he went crazy. He started talking about how much he hated Boothbay Harbor and the fishing community that ran the town. He said it was a fisherman that broke up him and my mother. He called her a whore; I ran out of the house. That was the night I called you from the Irving station. You and Meadow came to my rescue. You never pushed me to tell you what was going on; you just drove me to my mom's house and held me until I was ready to let go. I tried to ask my mother what Dad was talking about, but she wouldn't tell me."

Jack's only response was to hold her closer. He hunted in his mind for a way to change the subject, but Stephanie beat him to it.

"We have had all our...firsts... together, Jack. Even that short time in junior year when we broke up."

"That lasted a whole week, didn't it?" Jack asked sarcastically.

"Shut up, you deserved it by getting drunk and walking away from the party, leaving me to explain to your parents what happened. What we have is maybe what everyone calls puppy love, but it feels real enough for me."

"Me too."

JACK HAD A GOAL FOR himself; by the end of summer, he wanted to be in a real boat, not a skiff. He wanted to be able to fish trawl strings and fish all year. He would still go with his father, but it was time for him to grow as a lobsterman too. To help Jack reach his goal, Stephanie started keeping track of Jack's finances—not that he was irresponsible, but lobstering was a business, and Stephanie had learned a lot about what Jack could do to reduce his taxes. This also gave her the opportunity to deposit some of her own money into his savings account without him knowing; she knew her future was with Jack, and she considered it an investment. She was also still living with her mother and didn't have any bills other than her car. Jack had told her that Russell had started charging Jack rent the very next day after graduation. The funny thing was that Lucy had already told Stephanie that Russell did the same thing to her, but as soon as she got her own place, he gave Lucy back all the money she had ever paid.

This summer felt so different than the past summers. Other summers there was the security of going back to school, a familiar place, back to friends, and teachers that you knew. Both Stephanie and Jack had different feelings about this summer. Jack had a goal and a plan laid out; his only uncertainty was whether Mother Nature would cooperate with that plan. Would there be issues with bait or the price of lobster? His outboard had many hours on it and was a concern, though it started easily every morning. He had been searching for a bigger boat, but nothing was coming up in his price range. He knew his father was considering going to a new boat, but if his father sold *Wicked*, he would want top dollar for it, and Jack knew it was out of his range.

Stephanie found herself anxious all summer; she was ready to get college started and take on the new challenge. Her mother wasn't thrilled with the idea of her driving back and forth to Portland every day for school, but she wanted to stay in Boothbay Harbor and didn't want to pay to live an hour and a half away. Along with being anxious, she also wanted this summer to last forever. After this summer, it was the real world, well, as real as it can get for a college student.

It was mid-August when Stephanie, Jack, and Russell drove out to Harpswell so Jack could make the final purchase of his new boat. He had found a thirty-foot Repco with a one hundred and sixty-five horsepower, four-cylinder John Deere with around eight thousand hours on it. Jack and Russell had checked it out a week ago; they were both happy with the condition of the boat and engine. Jack was especially happy that the hull was already red; he liked his boat's name, *Red at*

Night, and wanted to name this one the same. *Red at Night* had proven to be a good and lucky name. Stephanie dropped them off at the dock, and after the bill of sale was signed and money had changed hands, or rather, a check, Jack and Russell headed for home. Jack had been in and out of Harpswell Harbor a number of times, but it always made him nervous; this time was worse because he wasn't in a small skiff with a short draft; he was in a full-size boat. Also, when he had been over here for the lobster boat races, there were plenty of boats to follow; today he didn't see anyone. He didn't want to put his new-to-him boat up on one of these jagged ledges. The boat did have a GPS, and the way out of the harbor was plotted on it. It also had a decent fathometer so he would be able to see how deep the water was.

Jack had saved enough money to buy the boat without financing, but in the interest of building a credit history, he financed half of the boat and used the other half of his savings for any immediate repairs or changes the boat needed. He also bought two hundred new traps. He rigged them into trawl strings. Most lobstermen fished five or six trap trawls, one trap on the rail and the rest across the stern, but since the stern of the Repco was so narrow, he rigged his as four trap trawls; one trap would be on the rail, and the other three would go back on the stern.

"Those four trap trawls will be great for Spring Cove at Squirrel Island; you'll be able to sneak them in amongst the moorings!" Russell said as he watched Jack rig the strings.

His plan was to fish the new *Red at Night* as much as he could for the next month, then haul out, make any changes and repairs, and then put it back in for the winter. This boat was keel-cooled, which meant that the engine's coolant circulated through copper pipes attached to the outside of the hull; that way the seawater would cool the coolant. It also had what was called a dry exhaust, which meant that the exhaust pipe came directly off the turbo and up through the cabin. This made the boat louder than having a wet exhaust, but it would provide some heat in the cabin this winter. He could get by with the electronics it had for now but would want to update them before summer. He would also add a CB radio; almost all lobstermen communicated via VHF, but Jack, his father, and a few others used CBs to communicate a little more secretly. It also helped Russell get in touch with Jack if he was in his truck.

Not long after Jack had bought his boat, Russell made the call to Arvid and Arvin Young to have them start laying up a thirty-three-foot Young Brothers hull. His thirty-foot South Shore was starting to feel small, and with the diesel engine he had put in just a year ago, it was prime time for selling. He always liked the looks of the Ernest Libby designs that the Young Brothers used to build their boats. The hulls had a low-profile hot rod look about them, which also matched their speed. Known to push easy, they had become the choice for racers and full-time lobstermen looking for efficiency. They also had a long history in the business and a good reputation.

Young Brothers had several different hulls to choose from, starting with their thirty-footer all the way up to their forty-six-footer. Russell had always liked the look of the Mark V, a thirty-three-footer he saw at the races. It was big enough so he could haul more traps comfortably, but not so big as to be cumbersome in some of the tight spots he fished.

The following spring, the *Old Smoke* was launched; the black hull reflected waves in the water; it had a silver strip just above the gray bottom paint. The name was in silver lettering too. Russell was some proud of his new boat. Everywhere he looked on the boat, there was a piece of his family. Jack had helped build it, and Lucy and Anne had lent a hand where they could. Anne framed a picture of the four of them standing beside the black hull the day it arrived and stuck it just beside the GPS unit so Russell could see it. He wouldn't lose this boat.

As time passed, Jack felt it was time to move out of his parents' house. Lucy had moved out a few years ago into his parents' old house on the "Finn Family Compound." He couldn't find a place in town that he liked or could afford. He was sitting at the dinner table looking at the real estate section when his father walked in.

"You buying a house?"

"No, trying to find a place to rent."

"Why, my house not good enough for you?"

"No, Dad, of course not. It's just that I am getting older now and need a little more privacy."

"I get ya. I wouldn't rent, though; why pay someone else's mortgage."

"Have you seen the prices of houses lately, Dad? I know I am doing well money-wise, but I don't want to get in over my head."

"Have you looked at land?"

"Yeah, but even land in this area is crazy."

By this time Russell had poured a cup of coffee and had sat down across from Jack. His pipe was stowed in his breast pocket, as Anne did not allow smoking in the house. He looked out the window over at some trees in the distance and stroked his chin. Jack lifted his head from the paper to look at his father, who was in deep thought.

"What are you thinking, Dad?"

"How about a quarter acre, with a water view, already has a driveway and the best possible neighbors?"

Jack turned his head to see what his father was looking at. Just to the side of the driveway there was a patch of trees, the same ones he had played in as a boy; he probably had a tree house out there still.

"Are you thinking about selling me that section between us and Mack Andrews?"

"Sure am; I will even make it a half-acre, and you can have clear to the shore."

"What is this going to cost me?"

"Twenty thousand, free lawn mowing, and free snow plowing for the rest of my... or your mother's days. You take care of Lucy's, too, until she is married. Oh, and you can't ever sell it; it needs to stay in the Finn name."

"Deal," said Jack with no hesitation.

"Okay, boy, I will talk to your mother, and we will draw up a contract. But you can get busy planning your house if you like."

"Yeah, I may even go as far as calling Hyson Construction and have them come take a look."

"That's not a bad idea; Gerald Hyson is an old friend of mine, and his two grandsons, Donald and Brian, are good guys as well. They will probably even let you help build it to keep the cost down. Jack, it would be smart to get Stephanie involved in this as well. I know you two are not married yet, but this could possibly affect her as well. Catch my drift."

"Caught, measured, banded, and in the tank!"

So, it began. Jack and Stephanie worked with Hyson Construction and an architect and designed a simple home that would complement the surrounding houses. Jack really didn't care about the floor plan; he just wanted a large back porch, and he wanted v-notch pine paneling throughout the house; he hated the look and feel of drywall. Stephanie insisted on an open kitchen and living room plan with a bathroom somewhere near the entryway; that way Jack wouldn't have to walk through the house all smelly to get to the shower.

While planning the house, they had discussed marriage and children. Both agreed they wanted to try living together for a while first; also, Stephanie wanted to get her career moving. Jack was planning to build a new boat soon and wanted to have the house and boat behind him before going further.

Stephanie was at work and was on the phone with Jack. His engine had broken down, and he had to be towed in. None of the local boatyards could spare their mechanics for at least three days or more. A lady walked in with short reddish hair; she looked to be in her thirties. She had a toddler in one hand and an infant in a carrier in the other. Stephanie cut her conversation off with Jack to talk to the lady.

"Hello, welcome to Mid-Coast Accounting. My name is Stephanie; did you have an appointment?"

"No, I wanted to drop off my husband's new business packet personally. I like to meet the people we are working with."

"Oh yes, Williams, right? Williams Mobile Marine. I will be handling that account myself. Do you have any questions?"

"No, we just need to get the ball rolling. He grew up here but has been gone for so long he is trying to get his foot back in the door."

"Ma'am, do you mind waiting a second while I make a phone call?"

Stephanie walked out of the reception area to a back office; she was gone just for a moment and came back.

"Have your husband call this number; he is my boyfriend, Jack Finn; he has a four-cylinder John Deere in his lobster boat that just died. The boatyards are telling him three days to look at it.

"I will, thank you very much. My name is Abigail, by the way."

"Nice to meet you, Abigail, and who may these two be?"

"This one is Lizzy," she motioned to the toddler standing up, sucking her thumb but with beautiful blue eyes locked in on Stephanie. "And this little guy is Josh."

"They are beautiful, Abigail. I know we just met, but if you ever need someone to watch these two, let me know."

"I will, thank you."

Stephanie went to Jack's after work; she figured she could help with the house, if possible; if not, she would check in with Anne to see if she needed help getting dinner ready. She noticed a couple of strange vehicles as she was coming in the driveway; one was a service truck with no logo on the side, the other a Jeep Grand Cherokee that had the obvious signs of belonging to someone with small children. She walked down to the dock and found Abigail sitting in a chair rocking the baby, whose name she remembered was Josh, while Jack was playing with the little toddler, Lizzy, on the dock.

"Well, nice to see you again so soon," said Stephanie.

"Yes, Michael sent me for parts, and this place is so nice, and Lizzy seems to love Jack; we decided to hang out for a while," Abigail responded.

Lizzy squealed with laughter at a funny face Jack was making at her.

Stephanie walked a little further and saw a man with a dirty ball cap on; it was so dirty she couldn't make out the logo. He was mumbling to himself as he worked, sometimes mumbling and sometimes singing some random song.

"Michael, don't be rude; say hi to our new accountant and possible new babysitter," Abigail said, while holding Josh up so he was standing on her legs while she supported him.

"Babysitters... we are a team; I will play with them, and Stephanie can change the diapers," said Jack.

"Doesn't work that way, brother, sorry to say. Hi Stephanie, I am Michael."

"Hello Michael, nice to meet you. How is it going?"

"I have a few more things to tighten up, then we can take it out and run it. I think you will be all set, though; I am just anal and don't like to walk away from something until I have seen it run."

Russell and Anne walked down to the dock as well, and they all sat and talked while Michael finished up the engine. Russell joined Jack in entertaining Lizzy while Anne couldn't help but hold little Josh.

Michael hit the starter button, and the little John Deere diesel came to life. Michael looked over the engine constantly, making sure there were no leaks. He was also making a mental list of what future maintenance would be coming up that he could get Jack to agree to. As soon as the engine was up to temperature, Jack and Michael headed out of the cove to give the engine a test run. Russell had Stephanie, Anne, Abigail, Lizzy, and Josh along for a boat ride in the *Old Smoke*.

Michael seemed to lose all personality when he was focused; he didn't say please or thank you; he just told Jack what he wanted. He didn't bark out orders, but you could tell he wanted them done, and he spoke quickly.

"Up two hundred RPMs... up another 200... good, up another 200." Michael ordered while inspecting not only the engine now but the boat as a whole.

After reaching full throttle for a short time, Michael had Jack throttle down and go into reverse and back down hard, then had him do a series of turns while at as much throttle as Jack felt safe doing.

"It feels like you are out of alignment a little, and you may need a cutlass bearing soon. Your rudder has some slop in it as well. When my wife does up the bill, she will give you estimates for all that. Just know I err on the side of caution with my estimates and tend to go high." Michael said over the now-idling engine.

"Everything good over there?" Jack heard his father ask over the CB radio.

"Yeah, Dad, we just finished up; we are gonna put the engine box on and head back to the dock." Jack answered back.

"Negative, there is a plan brewing over here about cruising the harbor a bit and grabbing a bite to eat at Brady's. Stephanie wants you to come over here and pick her up. Lizzy wants a ride in her "new uncle Jack's boat."

"Uncle Jack," Jack said to himself in his head... I like the sound of that. Jack turned the boat towards his father and came alongside. Stephanie climbed aboard while Russell picked up Lizzy and passed her over to Michael. Michael decided to stay with Lizzy on Jack's boat, but Lizzy seemed pretty content hanging out with Stephanie. Jack even set up a box for her to stand on so she could run the boat.

From that afternoon on, the Williams family and Finn family became close friends. Jack and Stephanie babysat for them often, and the Williamses started coming over for Finn family breakfast, which gave Michael a chance to meet Clive and start building up some contacts. Jack liked having an older person for a friend—someone not his dad, but another guiding voice, like an older brother. Michael was on the bossy side, but Jack figured that was some of the Navy veteran coming out. Michael didn't talk much about his time in the service, and Jack didn't push. Michael did take Jack shooting, and Jack was impressed with how good of a shot Michael was. They both enjoyed having a cold beer on Jack's back porch and just talking about life.

CHAPTER ELEVEN
Lucy and Sam

LUCY, BEING BUILT A LITTLE more husky than other women, was at a great advantage when she played sports. She was known as "The Wall" in field hockey and soccer. She wasn't overweight; she ate a normal diet; she could run and keep up with the other girls, but she was also much stronger. Her female classmates loved her and were always nice to her; the boys, on the other hand, were horrible. One boy asked if she had her own area code; one even accused her of being a boy in a dress. She was surprised when a boy asked her to prom but was upset when she learned that her friends paid him to ask her and to go with her. She never told them that she found out.

The current dating scene for Lucy was much like it was in high school; boys, now men, didn't ask out girls who were taller than them or had a bigger build. She tried to be flirty, hoping her personality would shine past her figure, but it never seemed to work. She remained her flirty, funny self in hopes someone would see her for who she was.

Jack was having a cold beer with his father out on the lawn that acted as a courtyard of sorts for the Finn Family compound. Lucy had driven in and was bouncing about and seemed to have a glow about her. She walked lively from her car down to where they were.

"What has you all giddy?" asked Russell

"Do you remember me talking about the guy at work? Well, we started talking about stuff, and I told him about MacIntyre's; he sounded interested, so he will be meeting me there tonight."

"Good for you, Lucy; I can't wait to meet him." said Jack

"Don't go making a big deal of it; it's not a date, but I hope he likes spending time with me."

Jack and Russell paused, each not knowing how to say what they were thinking.

"Well, I am going to get a shower and change. I need to figure out what to wear."

Lucy walked away towards her house.

"Dad, that whole 'likes spending time with me' line didn't sit well with me. Am I being too protective?"

"Well, Jack, Lucy is really tough on the outside. Like an old hardshell lobster, but she isn't so confident on the inside. You see how she is; she is a big-framed girl. Most guys don't see her for who she is; they just see a large woman. She never had a single boyfriend through school; well, she had one, but you remember how that went. I think Lucy has a soft spot for anyone who shows her some attention. I think you have your hackles up because it's your sister, and you should listen to your instincts but play nice in the sandbox."

Jack nodded in agreement.

"Stephanie coming to MacIntyre's?" Russell asked after a moment.

"Yeah, I'm running the boat over; then she is going to meet me there."

Russell had remembered that Jack had taken a couple of sleeping bags down to his boat; he was pretty sure Jack and Stephanie would be sleeping out on the boat tonight.

Jack finished his beer and walked down to the boat. It was early, but he could just cruise slowly, and he would get to MacIntyre's at the perfect time. Jack never grew tired of the ocean. He had no problem taking a slow cruise by himself; it was like a form of meditation for him. Just the hum of his diesel engine, the smell of the sea, and knowing he was a part of this environment. He rounded Spruce Point and headed in past Tumbler Island. As he drew closer to MacIntyre's, he could see that his parents, Stephanie, and Lucy, had arrived before him. Upon laying eyes on the man standing next to Lucy, his hackles went up again. He was standing next to Lucy, but, if Jack didn't know any better, he was staring at Stephanie's butt. Jack tied up the boat and took a deep breath. "He wasn't staring; it just looked like he was staring," he tried to convince himself.

Jack walked up the ramp and went out to kiss Stephanie and let the kiss linger a little longer than normal.

"For Christ's sake, Jack, get a room!" said Lucy.

Stephanie blushed a little, but Russell gave him a look as if to say he knew what he was doing. Jack walked up to the young man standing next to Lucy. He was shorter than Jack and Lucy and built like a T-rex dinosaur with short, small arms.

"Hi, I am Jack, Lucy's brother," said Jack as he put his hand out for a handshake.

What Jack got in return was a half-hearted handshake with no eye contact, and something that sounded like "Trevor" was mumbled.

Jack's hackles were in overdrive now, but he maintained his composure and figured it would be best to step away for a second and talk with Stephanie.

While talking to Stephanie and his father, he kept an eye on Trevor; his whole demeanor was just off. He also told Lucy to get him a beer; while Lucy was gone, he would try to chat with the other girls hanging around. When Lucy came back, her mother stood beside her to talk to her and Trevor.

"Hey, I am hungry; go get me a burger or something," Trevor ordered Lucy.

Jack could see that Lucy was taken aback and on the fence of compliance and defiance, but she wasn't given the opportunity to choose.

"PLEASE," said Anne in a voice loud and sharp enough that everyone gave pause. "You will use manners when speaking to my daughter, or you will leave."

"I ain't fuckin leavin' till I am good and ready."

It was Jack's turn now.

"You will show a little more respect to my mother and sister."

"Fuck you, lobster boy, what are you going to do about it?"

As Russell looked on, he could see Jack get a funny half-grin on his face. Jack wasn't a fighter, but he had been working on lobster boats since he was six. Jack owned the moment.

The rail at Macintyre's was thirty-six inches high; though not in compliance with modern building codes for a dock, it had been grandfathered. This put the rail just above Trevor's hip. Jack took two steps and placed his hand in the middle of Trevor's chest. When Trevor grabbed onto Jack's arm, Jack reached down and grabbed one of Trevor's feet and pulled it towards him, then up. This caused Trevor to lose all balance, so he let go of Jack's arm and tried to grab for the rail, but it was much too late. He was already going over the rail and headfirst into the water below. He came to the surface swearing and started swimming to one of the closest docks. Jack jumped down onto a nearby dock, and when Trevor tried to pull himself up, Jack pushed him back into the water.

"Let me back up, motherfucker!" yelled Trevor.

"I will let you back up here on one condition: we fight. One-on-one, me and you on this dock. Nobody disrespects my sister and mother. You ain't fit to hold Lucy's hand, you piece of shit. Now come on up and fight or swim over to the shore and get out," said Jack, as he pointed to the shore nearby.

Jack took a couple of steps back to show he was willing to allow him back on the dock. Trevor didn't even make any consideration; he just started swimming off to the shore.

Jack walked up the ramp to applause, but he really didn't feel he deserved it. Stephanie wasn't clapping, mostly because she was comforting Lucy.

"Why can't I find a good guy? Why do I have to be built like a linebacker for the Patriots?"

"Lucy, you are a beautiful person, and any guy should be lucky to be with you. Don't sell yourself short," Stephanie said.

That night, while Jack and Stephanie were in the *Red at Night*, anchored just outside of Lobster Cove, they were both sitting on the engine box, leaning back, watching the rain fall.

"I have never seen that side of you before, Jack."

"Sorry you had to; maybe I went a little too far, but the way he was treating my sister, then swearing at my mother... that just didn't sit well with me."

"I don't think it was too far. Lucy knows without a doubt that you are in her corner, not that she ever doubted it. I just feel bad for her—not pity, just sad. She is such a great person, but because she doesn't fit the mold of "hot chick," guys don't see her for who she is".

"I get it; you are right; any guy would be lucky to have her."

"What about me, Jack? What if I looked like Lucy? Would you still like me?"

"Steph... when I first met you, I was a teenager, and you were a "hot chick," but the only reason we have made it this far, and the reason we will last until we are old and gray, is because we see so much more of each other than our physical appearances. I love you now, and I will love you when you are old. As for my sister, Lucy will find someone eventually; she is too good of a person not to share it with someone else."

Lucy was walking through the Hannaford, figuring out what she was going to cook herself for dinner, and almost as if by habit, she strolled close to the deli section. There had been a guy there that she liked, but since the Trevor incident, she was reluctant to try to talk to him anymore than their usual casual conversation.

SAM MARTIN WAS WORKING THE deli at Hannaford's when he saw her from a distance. It was the girl he had been talking to — well, trying to talk to or flirt with— but he wasn't sure he was getting the message across. He really wasn't sure if she was interested in him. She was such a nice person, and funny; he wasn't sure if she was that way with everyone or just him. Well, today would be the day he would find out.

"No holding back this time, Sam Martin," he said to himself under his breath, although he had said that to himself every time he had seen her since the first time he had talked to her. What if she didn't come over to the deli? What if she didn't need her thinly sliced turkey and provolone cheese? When was the last time she had gotten it? He couldn't remember. Should he go after her? Chase her down in the store? No, here she came with her big smile on her angelic face. Her auburn hair was down and cascading off her shoulders.

"Hi, I tried your sandwich, the thinly sliced turkey, provolone, cucumber, and mayo. You are right, it's the best summertime sandwich," said Sam in an effort to start a conversation.

"Good, I am glad you liked it," answered Lucy.

"Um...I," Sam faltered as his nerves kicked in. He had this rehearsed in his head, but now the words were stuck. "Come on, Sam, get your shit together and ask the girl out," he said to himself. "How would you like to go to dinner with me tomorrow night?" he blurted out almost in one continuous word.

"I would love to."

"Um...ok. May I pick you up at your place?"

"That would be nice," Lucy said, wondering if she should warn him that it would more than likely be a family affair. She jotted down her address and phone number on a piece of waxed paper.

The next evening, Lucy was outside with Jack and her parents, patiently waiting for Sam to show up. She could see that Jack was a little tense. He never stopped being a brother. Sam pulled in, and she could tell he felt a little odd being under the scrutiny of four pairs of eyes. He got out and walked over, keeping his focus on Lucy. He walked up to her first and said hello and gave her a small peck on the cheek. He then greeted Anne, then Russell and Jack.

"At least this guy has manners," said Jack to himself.

They broke out into conversation about his work and how long he had lived in Boothbay Harbor and other small talk. With every word spoken, all parties felt more at ease.

Sam took Lucy to a restaurant in Brunswick, and then they went bowling afterwards. Sam didn't want to sit in silence and watch a movie; he wanted to talk and have a conversation. He wanted to know this girl. On the way home, Lucy asked Sam to pull into a small parking lot across the street from the Catholic church. It was the Lost at Sea Memorial, but it had the best view of the harbor. It was dark, but the moonlight made the waves in the harbor sparkle.

"How is it possible a beautiful, funny, smart girl like you is still single?" Sam asked.

"Probably because I am built like a semi-truck," Lucy said with an insecure laugh.

"Really, I hadn't noticed. I have been watching you for a while. You have a smile that could light up the darkest of days and a twinkle in your eye that, well, just makes me feel good when I look at you. I really like you, Lucy Finn; I hope you know that."

Lucy had a frog in her throat and couldn't speak, but she had to do something. She leaned forward and kissed Sam, placing one hand gently on the side of his head.

"That's how I feel, Sam."

When Sam pulled into the Finn Family compound, Jack was sitting outside drinking a beer and thumbing through his phone. Sam had gotten out and opened her door, and she could see Jack nod with approval from the distance, even though he was trying to make it look like he wasn't watching.

Sam gave her another kiss and said goodnight. Lucy walked over to Jack and asked, "Where is Stephanie?"

"She went to bed already. I felt like staying up. Looks like things went well."

"He said I am beautiful, Jack; he said my smile could light up the darkest of days and that my eyes twinkle and make him feel good."

"You are beautiful, Lucy. Always have been. I am glad you found someone who told you so. I hope it works out between you two."

"I think it will, Jack; I think it will."

CHAPTER TWELVE
The New Boat

"I CHRISTEN THE *RED AT Night*!" With that, Anne Finn swung the champagne bottle so hard it would have impressed Babe Ruth. The bottle broke on contact with the fiberglass hull. The scribed glass may have helped it break, but Anne really didn't need the help. She was a rugged and seasoned Maine woman, a breed apart from other women. Her constant shaking of the bottle beforehand ensured the bubbly fluid would spray everywhere, including on her. Jack had considered having his girlfriend christen the boat, but his mother had done the past two, both having been good boats with good luck; also, Stephanie wanted to be onboard for the first ride. Anne hopped off the trailer, and Dave Burt from Liberty Marine slowly backed the trailer down the boat ramp. As soon as the bottom of the boat was wet but not yet floating, Dave gave Jack the thumbs-up for him to start the engine. This was to ensure that the raw water pick-up was in the water.

Jack had already started the engine a week ago, but he was still nervous something could go wrong. He turned the key to arm the ignition. The engine box was off so he could hear the fuel pump kick on and other electronically controlled gadgets come to life. He closed his eyes and hit the start button.

The thirteen-liter diesel engine roared to life. The sound was deep and throbbing, almost as if the engine was surging, as if it was anxious to crawl out of the engine compartment and attack. But soon it smoothed out to a consistent, smooth idle. He looked back to his best friend and mechanic, Michael Williams, who sold him the engine. Michael had his head over the port side of the boat, making sure the engine was pumping water out of the exhaust. Michael turned to him and gave him a thumbs-up. He turned and looked at Stephanie, who was sitting in a tall helm chair, holding a grab handle mounted to the bulkhead; he was awarded a warm smile of approval. He looked through the windshield of the boat at Dave and gave him an "okay" sign. Dave backed the trailer in further, and *Red at Night* was officially launched. He pulled the shift lever back to the reverse position, and the boat lurched backward. Jack grinned at the sheer power of the engine and how quickly his boat responded.

"That is going to take some getting used to; the last *Red at Night* didn't jump like that!" He chuckled out loud.

He shifted into forward, and the boat lurched again. The engine changed tempo momentarily with the added load of shifting but settled quickly. He turned the wheel hard to starboard and moved the throttle up slightly. *Red At Night* made a tight turn to starboard and then headed straight as Jack turned the wheel back. He looked back at Michael, who was opening every hatch and checking everything over.

"Everything is good. My laptop is hooked up already. Bring her up in two hundred rpm increments; Steph, mind doing me a favor? When you see this box turn green, click it. That will log the data for that RPM. Once you click it, give me a thumbs up, and then I will give Jack the okay to go up another 200. I will keep walking around and keeping an eye on everything. Jack, keep an eye on the gauges, please," Michael commanded.

Stephanie turned the laptop towards her; she had grown accustomed to Michael's bossy military nature. She looked over the laptop screen at Jack; this was a big day for him. Jack and his father had been working on this boat for several months. He had ordered it as a bare hull, no motor, shaft, cabin, or deck. Over the winter, they had put it all together. The engine was a 13-liter Scania, bought from his best friend Michael, who was now running the sea trial on it. Jack had spent a little extra on this boat, having a small bathroom, or head, as it is called in the marine world. Stephanie had told him for all the money he was spending, there should be no need for her to have to use a five-gallon bucket. Other than the head, it had the normal features of a high-end commercial lobster boat. A large bed or berth in the bow, rather than two V-berths, and he had a custom mattress made for it. Everything was painted white with what Jack called "gel coat." There was a small closet built around all the mechanicals against the bulkhead to help keep the forward area clean and free of fumes.

She clicked the green box and gave Michael a nod. He gave a quick glance around the engine, then gave Jack the go-ahead to increase the engine's RPMs another two hundred. The boat surged forward, and the engine purred a little louder. Stephanie, Michael, and Jack continued the process all the way up to full throttle.

"30 knots on the GPS, Michael!" Jack said while the *Red at Night* sailed through the water.

Michael glanced at the laptop briefly. "You are a little light on load, so I think you can add another inch of pitch to the propeller and get another knot out of her. If you want to bump it up to the recreational rating for the races, I will have a race prop made with another two inches of pitch."

"What do you mean, recreational rating?" Stephanie asked.

"This engine is sold commercially at six hundred and seventy-five horsepower. For recreational use, it's sold at eight hundred. I can flash the engine's ECU up to the recreation rating for the races, then flash it back after he is done. But he needs more pitch in the propeller to take advantage of the extra horsepower. Jack, I am going to take one more look around and see if I can find anything."

Michael found no leaks, and nothing was "out of spec" on the computer. Michael explained that all the data collected would be sent to the engine manufacturer, and they would "sign off" on the warranty. Jack slowed the boat down while Michael packed up his laptop and other tools. Stephanie looked around at the interior of this area called the cockpit. One area Jack spent a lot of money on was his electronics. There were several places local to him, but he chose to purchase everything from a friend in New York that called himself Wharf Rat. Wharf Rat had outfitted him with radar, GPS, and sonar, all top-of-the-line Furuno. The inside of the cockpit was painted in white gel coat, and the deck was a haze gray, a nod to Michael's days in the Navy.

Stephanie looked back at Jack, who was staring out of the open window in the windshield. He had a brand-new black Scania hat on; he joked that he had bought the hat and the engine came free; his brownish blonde hair stuck out around the sides and back and curled up a little. He had sported that look since high school. Soon, when the summer sun hit his hair, it would turn even more blond. His blue eyes partially squinted as the sun was burning through the spring fog. He was wearing the typical hooded sweatshirt, a staple among Maine lobstermen; this one was a Pemaquid Lobster Boat Races sweatshirt from last year. It was still considered a "good" hoodie as opposed to the "work" hoodies that had more time, stains, or holes. With Jack, it was stains. Jack was one of the messiest eaters she had ever known. He had on a clean pair of blue jeans and his clean sneakers.

Jack could feel Stephanie's eyes on him; she did that often, not staring but looking. Even this moment of launching his new boat, this boat he had dreamed about since Billy Hallinan brought the first 38 Young Brothers to Boothbay Harbor, didn't trump the feelings she had for him and that he had for her. When he felt her eyes move off him, he looked at her from the side of his eye. Her cheeks were red from the fresh, cool spring air. Her brunette hair was loose, with strands of hair dancing in the wind. She had one of his flannel shirts on with the sleeves rolled up and only half buttoned up to reveal a long-sleeved shirt underneath. He knew she had a long-john shirt on under that as well. Stephanie would rather wear fourteen layers than wear a coat. She was wearing black yoga pants, the ones Jack liked. He grinned and looked a little longer, only to get caught by her turning back to him. He tried to play it off, but it didn't work. Her facial expression clearly said, "I know you were looking and what you were thinking... you have to wait."

Jack refocused his attention on navigating the boat up into Lobster Cove, where his family's property was. The "Finn Family Compound," they called it. At the shore was a dock house built upon a small wharf with a ramp that led down to a dock. Jack turned the boat and backed in close to the dock to tie up. Up on the wharf, there were several people gathered to celebrate the launch of the new boat. Launching parties are a custom started back in the B.C. era with the Egyptians, Greeks, and Romans, who drank wine to honor the gods. In Maine, in modern times, everyone gathered for rum, beer, and food.

"My wife made a whole plate of them deviled eggs, and I am going to get some before all of them gulls up there eat them all," Michael said, gesturing at the crowd up on the wharf. Then he jumped out of the boat, onto the dock, and ran up the ramp.

"I will go up and help your mother and see if she needs anything, though with Abigail, Lucy, and my mom up there, she is probably all set," Stephanie said.

Jack turned off the boat and gave a quick look around, then turned to Stephanie. "Yeah, I am going to go up and throw some food down my grocery hole and have a beer. I gotta give a few boat rides too. If anyone asks you, you tell them it went twenty-eight knots, ok?"

"You guys and this racing drama—you're worse than those Real Housewives shows. Just make sure you save the last boat ride for me, okay?"

"Yes, Ma'am!"

Jack helped Stephanie out of the boat and went up the ramp to the party. Lucy's boyfriend, Sam, was at the top of the ramp, and Jack decided to talk with him while Stephanie went to help his mother.

"Sam, I got to say thank you for all your help with ordering the food. Mom said you saved me a bunch of money," said Jack.

"It was nothing; you helped me out with that spare tire that time; now I can say we are even."

"Hey, I am just some glad you met my sister. She had a couple of losers along the way. I tossed one guy overboard."

"Oh, I know; that story is a part of Boothbay Harbor history. It's a good thing I didn't hear it before I asked Lucy out. Jack, your sister is just a great person, and man, does she love you and is proud of you."

Jack blushed a little and nodded. Lucy had now walked over.

"What are you two talking about?" Lucy asked.

"Just how big of a pain in the ass you are, and how big of a nag you are," jested Jack.

"You're the pain, little brother, always have been." She stopped and looked down at Jack's boat. "The boat looks great, Jack. You and Dad did an awesome job. I really like that red."

"Thanks, sis."

Jack gave a few boat rides while everyone ate and drank. As the day went on, it seemed that Stephanie became more distracted. He could tell something wasn't right, but didn't want to press. When the party ended, Jack and Stephanie headed out for a nice, quiet boat ride for just the two of them.

The next morning, Jack woke up to an empty bunk in his new boat. This confused him greatly because he had tied off to a mooring just outside of Lobster Cove. He tossed on his boxers, pants, and t-shirt. He couldn't find his hoodie anywhere. He went out on deck, and through the windshield windows, he saw Stephanie's bare legs. He climbed up the port side along the cabin and saw her, bundled up in his hoodie, staring out into the morning fog.

"You ok?" Jack asked as he sat down beside her.

"Yeah... no... I don't know."

"What is wrong?"

"The night before last I was checking in on my mother; she had been talking to my dad on the phone. You know how that goes. She was crying, and when I tried to comfort her, she told me to sit down... Jack... I don't even know how to say this next part. My dad isn't my father. I knew my mom had cheated on him, but I never thought he wasn't my dad."

"Well, then who is your father?"

"She said she can't tell me, not yet; she wants a chance to talk to him first, but I know she won't."

"Have you talked to your dad since?"

"Yes, but he won't tell me either; he says it's her punishment to have to look me in the face and tell me what kind of trash she slept with."

Jack didn't know what to say; what could someone say? Rob Turner had always been so cool, but also protective. Never a hint that he wasn't her father. He was curious about how he found out, but this wasn't the time or the place to play investigator. His parents had warned him since childhood that no matter how good a lie was told, the truth would always come to the surface. The longer the lie went on, usually the more pain it would cause when the truth came out. The thing was, though, the pain wasn't isolated to just the liar; it was now hurting an innocent bystander.

"Steph, I can't promise you we will never fight or argue. We have already had some minor ones through the years, but I do know you would never cheat on me, and you know I would never cheat on you. We will never cause the mess your parents have caused. Rob was your father for years; he went to all your games; he was always there for you and was always proud of you. Remember that, and if he chooses to fade away, that's on him. I won't, and my family won't."

She smiled at him, and she kissed him almost as if to say, "I know."

"The fog looks like it's clearing. Want to give Ebbtide a call and see if we can pick up breakfast to go?" Stephanie asked.

"Yes, that sounds like a good idea."

Later that evening, Jack and Stephanie were at Michael and Abigail's house. Michael and Jack were out in the shop talking over a couple of beers.

"So, you two have been together since high school; you live together; don't you think it's about time to, you know..." asked Michael, making a questioning motion with his hands.

"I am thinking and planning. I have started saving some money off to the side for a ring. I just launched the boat; her career is still growing, and she still hasn't moved into my place officially."

"Oh, bullshit, I know she has been living at your house for years now; what you mean is she hasn't finally moved everything from her mother's house to yours."

"Okay, okay, you got me there. We just like to take things slow. I am going to start putting away some money for a ring."

"You just be sure to bring me along when you are ready to buy."

A couple of months later, Jack and Michael went ring shopping. Jack carried the ring around in his truck or in his pockets, waiting for the right time. He decided he would do it on the 4th of July on his boat, under the fireworks.

CHAPTER THIRTEEN
Drive Safe

"TOMMY MACINTYRE!...HOW...WHY..." STEPHANIE screamed at her mother.

"Your father and I had an argument; I left the house and went to Macintyre's for a drink. Tommy was at the bar and saw I was upset. We started talking, dancing, and drinking more. We went up to his office." She stopped to take a breath; she clenched her hands into fists and then slowly relaxed. "I woke up the next morning; I came home, and your father — well, he wasn't home. We made up about the argument, but I didn't tell him about Tommy, but it ate me up inside. Shortly after you were born, we were both drunk and arguing. I told him that I had slept with someone else. We got divorced not long after; even after the divorce, he continued to ask who. I let it slip once that it was a fisherman and what night it happened. He started to figure things out; he took some of your hair that was on a brush at his house. As soon as he had the results, he called me and made me tell him," her mother finished.

Stephanie was dumbstruck; her biological father was one of the biggest sleazeballs in Boothbay Harbor. She felt dirty; her skin, her body, and her core felt tainted.

"Does Tommy know?" Stephanie asked.

"Oh God, no, what difference would that make?"

Stephanie didn't have an answer for that; what difference would it make? It's not like Tommy would be happy or start being a model citizen.

"I don't know what to say or do. I am paying for a mistake you made years ago." The anger in her was welling up, beyond the point of control. She felt the words coming, but the little voice in her head that was saying "don't say that" wasn't strong enough. "I hate you," Stephanie said as she walked out of her mother's house. It chilled her to the bone the way she said it. She didn't scream or yell it but said it cold and steady.

She found herself driving around Boothbay Harbor, Boothbay, East Boothbay, and Southport. There were so many things on her mind. She was wondering when Jack would propose; it seemed imminent; everything was in place. She had a job; Jack had his boat finished and in the water. They were both making good money. Why was he waiting? What was he waiting for? She had talked to Abigail about having Michael give Jack a little nudge. Has that happened yet? She knew Jack would be coming in soon, getting the boat washed and ready for tonight. It was the Fourth of July, and they always went out and cooked burgers and hotdogs on the grill, then watched the fireworks. She couldn't get out on that boat soon enough. Out on the water, with Jack, and away from all this... whatever it was.

Tommy MacIntyre was sitting in his office, feet up on the desk. He had just done a line of cocaine and was now smoking a joint. He was reveling in his newfound success; he had been trying to get into the drug-dealing scene for a while, as he knew there was lots of money to be had. He had learned about a guy in Portland, but when the Russians, who said they were from Boston, approached him, he decided he would make his move. He wanted to start slowly, and they had done that for a while, but lately they were starting to get pushy. They wanted to move entire trucks-full, using his place as a terminal of sorts, giving Tommy some product and cash. Casmiere, one of the Russians, would be driving a truck up tonight. Then other trucks from other places in Maine would be coming during the week to pick up "product," or as they nicknamed it, "lobster." Everything was moved as if it were lobster, in crates and totes. The trucks even had seafood restaurant logos on them. Things were going perfectly, and nothing seemed to be standing in his way.

"You okay? You seem very distant," Jack asked as he helped Stephanie onto the boat.

"I will tell you about it later. I just want to relax and let the world slip away. I do have a little disappointment for you, though. I can't go home with you tonight. I need to go see my mother after this is over. I don't want to talk about it right now, but I do need to talk to her tonight."

"No problem, I understand. Lucy and her new boyfriend, Sam, are going with Mom and Dad. They should be around the corner of Spruce Point soon. I would have gone back home after hauling, but it didn't make much sense."

"Okay, I am going to go up and use the bathroom before we go."

Stephanie hopped out of the boat and walked up the ramp at MacIntyre's Lobster. After using the bathroom, she heard Tommy's voice. She had known, or known of, Tommy MacIntyre for years, but she wanted to see him up close; she wanted to see if he looked anything like her. Everyone always said she looked like her mother, but she just had to look. As she rounded the corner by the bait shed, she started hearing two voices. One was definitely Tommy's, but the other had an accent. What she heard next made her gasp.

"Mr. MacIntyre, I am leaving you with roughly five hundred thousand dollars' worth of cocaine, marijuana, and hash. If anything should happen to it or you should get greedy with your share, there will be repercussions. Do you understand?" she heard the Russian man say.

"Yeah, I understand...," said Tommy.

"Just to be sure you do, here is a sample of what may come if you cross us."

She heard two strikes, as if a boxer was hitting a punching bag.

"Nothing personal," said the Russian, then she heard footsteps leading away.

Once she was sure the Russian was gone, she went to check on Tommy.

"Stephanie Turner? What are you doing here? What did you hear?" Tommy growled.

"I heard everything, and for reasons I can't explain, I am going to give you a chance to make this right. You have until tomorrow morning to contact the police. If you don't do it by then, I will. You understand me?"

"Why...why not call them yourself now?"

"Because it will be better for you if you do it, and maybe the police can use you to get the dealers."

"Okay, but why give me the chance?"

"Because I have something to tell you, and if you want to find out what that is, you will call the police yourself."

Stephanie turned and walked away. He sat there, catching his breath and thinking about everything that had just happened. These Russians were no joke; they would hurt him if he messed up, maybe even kill him. All the money in the world wouldn't do him any good if he was found dead floating in one of his lobster tanks, or would they stuff him in the steamer tank? He started to get up and go to his office. He would call Sergeant Nick Upham; Nick had known him for a while and would go easy on him.

He got up from his desk and heard Jack's boat backing away from the dock. He could see Stephanie, sitting up on top of the cabin, looking so high and mighty; she was such a goody-two-shoes, hey, but her mother wasn't, though. Why should he report himself? Maybe he should call the Russians. They would rough up Stephanie and maybe Jack Finn; maybe he would be able to watch as they roughed them up. That would be something to watch— Boothbay Harbor's dream couple getting smacked around. He looked for the number that he had been given to call in an emergency. Once he found it, he dialed it on his phone. The female voice that he lusted for, but feared, answered.

"Privet." The voice said.

Tommy, confused because he didn't know that she had just said hello in Russian, paused, trying to figure out what to say. They had only spoken a few times, but she was no joke and not to be messed with.

"Yes, this is to..." He tried to speak but was cut off by her yelling at him.

"No names, you durak. What is the problem? Why you call this number?"

"We were seen, Casmiere and I; a local girl saw us. She knows everything. She told me to go to the police, or she would in the morning."

"What is the girl's name?"

"Stephanie, Stephanie Turner."

"Well, it looks as though this Stephanie has made a mistake."

Tommy let out a sigh of relief; he was about to tell them about Jack when the Russian lady spoke again.

"Kill her."

Tommy heard the words and knew what she said.

"What?

"KILL...HER," the Russian lady said in loud, drawn-out words.

"I can't kill her. I am not a murderer."

"Then I have Casmiere kill you both, her quickly, you slowly, her first so you can watch."

"No, I will do it; she will be coming back to my dock later."

"Good, I will have Casmiere watch; let me know if you do it or not." Then she hung up.

Tommy's face felt numb, and he felt a painful tingling all over. What had he just agreed to do? He had to kill Stephanie Turner, the pride and joy of Boothbay Harbor. She wasn't just popular in school; anyone who met her loved her. "Maybe I should call Nick now?" he asked himself. No, Casmiere was probably already watching. If the police showed up, he would be a dead man. He had to do it; he had to kill her; he had come too far; there was so much more money to be made.

JACK AND STEPHANIE SAT NEXT to each other, holding each other's hands. Jack sensed Stephanie was distant all night, like she was thinking of something else. He knew just what to do to get her attention.

Stephanie had been trying to get herself to relax. She had a couple of beers but wanted to stop there because she knew she would have to drive to her mother's house tonight and apologize, then in the morning talk to Tommy. She looked over to see Jack reaching into his pants pocket. "Oh no, Jack, not tonight," she thought to herself, but then she thought a little harder. "Why not tonight? With all this crap in her life, she needed something stable.

She started to get butterflies as the thoughts of Jack getting down on one knee during the fireworks streamed in her head.

It was perfect; they were out of earshot from everybody, and everyone else on the boats tied up next to them were busy watching the fireworks.

She could feel Jack freeze, then shrug. The ring was not in his pocket; he must have left it in his truck or at home. She wasn't even sure he had a ring yet; oh well, he would eventually, and when he asked, it would be perfect. They would start making a family as soon as they were married. She knew she was getting ahead of herself, but she was ready, ready for the rest of her life with Jack Finn. She slid closer to him and rested her head on his shoulder.

Russell and Anne looked over at Michael and Abigail, wondering what had happened. They were sure Jack would make his move tonight; they were sure he went into his pocket for the ring. Both couples shook their heads in confusion.

After the fireworks, Jack pulled into MacIntyre's and tied up the boat. He walked her up the ramp and swore he saw Tommy looking down at them from his office window.

"Hey Steph, I know you are staying at your mother's tonight, but why don't I drive you. You did have a couple of beers."

"Jack, you are the lightweight in this relationship, not to mention I need to think on the way home."

"Are you sure you are all set to drive?"

"Yes, Jack. I will call you when I get home, just to make you feel better."

"Okay," he said, then bent down to kiss her. "Drive safe."

PART TWO
MELISSA'S STORY

CHAPTER ONE
The Dreamer and The Carpenter

The Dreamer

HER FATHER JUST DIDN'T UNDERSTAND her; she knew she could make it if she could just get there. He wanted her to keep doing local plays and musicals, hoping a talent scout would stumble upon her. She had no time for that; Hollywood moved too fast. She was already twenty-one; Julie Andrews, her favorite actress, was eighteen when she hit Broadway. No, she had to leave here, leave these cornfields, leave Walnut Creek, Ohio, and never ever look back.

To be sure her father wouldn't find her, she had said she was going to New York City to audition for a play, and she would be back in a few days. She had told her boss the same thing. It wasn't too farfetched; she had just had a starring role in a musical at the Ohio State Theater not long ago, and there were some people there from the Lincoln Center Theater. The rumor was that they had asked the director for contact information for some of the actors. But they hadn't called her or anyone else she knew.

She took a cab to the bus station with a single suitcase filled with as much as she could put into it. She had thought about buying a plane ticket, but that was expensive, and she didn't know how long it would take to get a job; she didn't even know where she was going to live. Instead, she decided to take a bus to Cleveland, then a train to Hollywood. Fifty-three hours on a train, but it would only cost a couple of hundred dollars.

The time on the train was torture: smelly people, dirty stations, and she didn't dare go to sleep. She dozed off a couple of times but woke up in a panic, checking for her purse, which she kept clutched close, much like a toddler with a teddy bear. She thought of her father; sometimes it brought a tear to her eye. That man had sacrificed so much, all the money he had put into her singing, acting, and dancing lessons. Since her mother had died, he had raised her. He enlisted help from some of his female friends as she got older and into maturity, but he was always there. A rock, a pillar, a piling in a rushing tide. She would make this right; she would make it big and buy him a new tractor for the farm; hell, if she made it big enough, she would buy the farm from the bank. He probably could have done it already if not for the money he spent on her.

Buckley Cooligan, or as his friends called him, Buck, was driving as fast as he felt he could get away with on his way home to see his daughter. He had decided to drive out to the Ohio State Theater to see if those bigwigs from New York had called. As it turned out, they had been trying to reach his daughter, Allison, but she wasn't picking up the phone. He didn't know why he was driving so fast; it's not like the paper he had written the contact info on was going to burst into flames. He just felt this was it; this was her big chance. She was the only one they had asked about.

He saw the train coming and stepped on the gas. He thought he could make it.

"Shit!" he yelled as he slammed on the brakes; the safety arms were coming down, and even though he could have kept going and probably would have made it, he changed his mind and decided to stop.

Unfortunately, the driver of the eighteen-wheeler behind him had not been paying attention. He had looked up and saw the pick-up moving right along and decided it was a good time to open a tube of Pringles. When he finally found them and opened them, he saw the railroad crossing lights and then the brake lights of the previously speeding truck. He slammed both feet down instinctively, one on the clutch and the other on the brake. He pushed himself against the back of his seat so hard he felt like it was going to rip it off its mounts. But all that effort was futile; he knew it too. The front bumper of his semi slammed the back tailgate of Buck's truck hard, so there is a chance Buck may have died before his truck even went out in front of the train; if he didn't, the brutal impact of the train certainly killed him.

Allison got off her train and walked up to a pay phone to call her father. She intended to lie and say she was calling from New York. They didn't have caller ID out on the farm, so there was no way for him to know. Other than not having caller ID, they also didn't have an answering machine; oh well, she would try again in a couple of days. Who knows, maybe in a couple of days she would already have a part in a movie and be able to fly home and tell him, or better yet, fly him out here and surprise him.

It turned out it was going to take more than a couple of days to get noticed. She had been in Hollywood for a week; she had spent the last two nights sleeping out on the streets. She was completely broke, and she decided it was time to concede and ask her father for help. She had been trying to call the house with no luck; she finally decided to call a neighbor to see if they knew where her dad was. The sound of the neighbor's voice was music to her ears; finally, she would be able to get ahold of her father, and he would send her some money so she could get back home.

"Your father is gone." Those words kept repeating in her head, over and over again, haunting her. She had no lifeline, no help now. She would not let his death or her betrayal of him go unwarranted. Come hell or high water, she was going to make it. She knew the bank owned most of the farm; there was no reason to go back; he had already been buried.

She found work waiting tables at a chain restaurant. Soon, she started looking for fancier restaurants closer to Hollywood, closer to where the talent, or people looking for talent, would be. She made a few friends and moved into a two-bedroom apartment with three other girls. It was less than ideal, but splitting rent and the other bills four ways made it worth it. All of them had similar dreams of stardom and helped each other. They made a pact: if one made it, they would help out the other three.

As time marched on, the four girls ended up going in different directions. Two gave up and headed back to whatever corner of America they had come from. The other ended up getting a good job at a bank and was able to move out and live on her own. Allison stuck with waitressing, and any free moment she had, she was looking for acting parts. She took parts in small local theaters to build up her acting resume. She scored a few roles in some commercials and was now making enough to hire an agent. She felt like she was finally making some progress, making up for running out on her father.

Sometimes the memory of her father hurt her, a sharp pain to the core. She had the best of intentions coming out here; she wanted to be able to help him like he had helped her. She knew the only way she could ever make it right was to make it big.

She stayed committed to her goal; she didn't get mixed up with any men, even the one that promised to get her some screen time. No, she wasn't going to earn this on her back; that would not be what her father wanted. She was going to make it on her sheer talent, and that was that.

The Carpenter

"Listen, if you are looking to make a bunch of money in this business, you need to head south. The building season is longer, the houses are bigger, and the clients are richer. Little Valley will always be here," said Steve Berger, owner and operator of Berger Construction.

"You saying you don't want me here, Boss?" said Mitchell Malcom, a new, young carpenter that had been working for Steve a few years.

"No, you are one of my best guys; you show up early, and you're the last to leave. You are one of the fastest framers I have ever seen, and you are accurate. I can have you on the ground as a cut guy or have you driving a nail gun. You don't even mind being up high on staging." Steve paused while putting another rack of nails in his Bostitch framing nail gun. "But I can see you want to grow; you want to expand; you want to have a truck with your name on the side of it. I can't do that for you. I am a small outfit;

there is no need for a co-owner or VP or anything like that. You could go down south for a while and work for one of those big outfits putting up those mansions you see that Robin Leech going on about. Live small, save your money, then come back here and start your own business."

"I don't know; it sounds awfully risky."

"You are not married, you have no kids, and your parents, with all due respect, are gone. Rent out that house so you can always come back, and you will always have income. Look, Mitchell, losing you is the last thing I want, but you will never be more than a wood butcher here. Yeah, I may move you into interior finish, but that's not going to change your pay that much. You have a force, a drive that shouldn't be bottled up here with me."

Steve watched as the wheels turned in Mitchell's eyes. He would hate to lose this kid— well, young man. He was in his early twenties, but he had ambition, drive, and dreams. Steve would rather see the kid get some traction out on his own; then he would have another subcontractor to call if he ever needed him.

"Look, Mitchell, here is what I will do: I will have my wife, Kathy, make you up a resume. We will even help send out copies. I will pay you another dollar per hour until you hear back. If nobody down there wants you, you keep the dollar, and you keep working for me, and we never talk about it again. If... no, when one of those companies calls you, you go down there, you work your ass off, come back here, and start your own business. If I call you to sub for me, you give me a special rate, deal?"

"Deal."

They shook hands and continued framing the wall.

That evening Mitchell sat in his father's old rocking chair and looked out over the front lawn. He had never left this place before. His family had taken very few vacations, and those were usually just over a weekend. He could see one of the many treehouses he had built over the years; throughout his childhood he had peppered his parents' property with them.

He had a passion for building, not models or small things; he liked to build big things, practical things. He built a shed for his bicycle when he was eight years old and even put in shelves for spare tubes, an air pump, and an oil can. When he was twelve, he had built a garage for his dad. Then, as soon as he had his worker's permit, he worked with Steve Berger every summer until he graduated from high school.

Steve had taken over the father role when Mitchell's father had passed away of a heart attack, and then his mother followed two years later. He had been on his own for a while now. He sipped his ice-cold beer and looked at the empty rocking chair to his left. Sitting here in this rocking chair made him feel close to his mom and dad. He needed their guidance right now. Should he listen to Steve and head down to Hollywood? Why not?

"One year," he said out loud to the warm evening air. "I will go down for one year."

One week later he had a job lined up with an outfit just outside of Hollywood, along with a small apartment. The old nineteen seventy-two Ford was loaded with his tools and filled with gas. Steve Berger passed him an envelope full of cash, and when Mitchell passed it back, Steve said no, it was his last paycheck and a little extra. Steve and his wife would take care of the house and handle the renters. All Mitchell had to do was work hard and save his money.

New Pine Creek was just about as far north in California as you could get, so much so that half the town was in Oregon. The fastest way to Hollywood was to take 395

South. Mitchell decided that if he was going to spend almost twelve hours in his truck, he was going to enjoy the scenery. He took 395 as far as Alturas, and from there he made his way west until he was on Route 1 south. This route was going to take much longer, but he would be able to see some of the ocean and more of what California was about.

Between the altered route and the old Ford big-block V8 drinking gasoline like it was cherry cola, he decided to break the road trip into two days. He had no idea what town he was in when he stopped; he just found a place that had a beach, food, and restrooms. He wasn't sure if it was safe or not, but he was sure the double-barreled shotgun, a family heirloom that had been his great-grandfather's, that was hanging in the back window would make sure nobody would mess with him.

Having his dad's old truck and the old shotgun did give him a sense of security, as if his dad was there watching over him. If his dad were still alive, he was sure he would fully support this plan to head to Hollywood. Well, he really wasn't going to Hollywood; he was headed to Glendale, which was not far from Hollywood or Beverly Hills. He had found a small apartment above a couple's garage. His dad would have been all for it, a chance for Mitchell to go out and prove himself. He missed his parents so much. Steve and his wife, Kathy, did their best to fill in the void, but he and his parents had been close. Losing his father to that heart attack came as a surprise. His dad was in such good health, and the same with his mother; he was sure that the loss of his father was too much for her. She had never been right after he passed.

"Why am I dwelling on that?" he said to himself as he stared out the windshield onto the beach. He had his jacket stuffed under his head like a pillow and his legs bent so he could fit across the large bench seat, and it was almost comfortable. Tomorrow he would drive the rest of the way and move into his apartment; he would have to go out and get a bed and other things, but that would be fine. Then on Monday, he would start his new job: building a mansion in Beverly Hills. He didn't know who it was for, but that didn't matter. Mansions meant money, and he was already going to start at a higher hourly rate than he was making with Steve. The monthly rent he was charging for his house was double that of his apartment. Yup, in a year he would go back to New Pine Creek with a ton of experience and some start-up money. With that thought, he dozed off to sleep.

The apartment was much smaller than his house, but the studio layout helped it feel more open and less confined. The dark faux wood paneling made the apartment darker than he had liked, and he was sure that if he dropped any change, the pale green shag carpet would digest it, as the rug almost looked like it should be mowed rather than vacuumed. The landlords were a very nice older couple; all they asked was to keep the noise down and pay the rent on time. Mitchell spent the weekend settling in and learning the neighborhood.

His first week of work went well. He liked most of the people on the crew, and most seemed to like him. It was much different than what he was used to; Steve's crew only consisted of three or four guys, five at most. There had to be fifty people working here, sometimes even more if you counted the electricians or plumbers.

Mitchell was placed on a framing crew, framing walls and standing them up. These guys worked fast; he was considered fast back with Steve, but he was just average here. That was fine; he would just have to push a little harder, that's all.

Mitchell started to build a life; he saved his money and lived small. He enjoyed the work and the area. One Friday afternoon, after putting in a sixty-plus-hour workweek, he decided it was about time to treat himself to a nice dinner. He got himself cleaned up and put on some decent clothes and headed out to find a nice restaurant.

CHAPTER TWO
Mini golf, Ice cream, and Sacrifices

ALLISON WAS IN A GOOD mood; before coming to work, she had gotten a call from her agent that he had landed her an audition to be a guest on a very popular TV show. It could very well be her launching pad. The restaurant was busy but not hectic; it had a rhythmic flow about it.

"Allison, I just seated the hottest guy in all Los Angeles County at one of your tables!" said the hostess, who seemed to be bursting.

Allison tried to peek around the corner to see, "Which table? What does he look like?"

"He is the one with the Robert Redford hair, the Paul Newman eyes and smile, and a body that belongs to a statue."

By now the rest of the waitresses were looking out onto the floor and audibly swooning over the young man.

"Get yourselves together, girls. I have plans, and I can't let some...boy stop me from my goals. I will go take his order like anyone else."

As she walked over, he looked up from the menu in her direction. She felt as if a shockwave had spread through the restaurant. He was cute, he had a nice smile, and those eyes! His skin looked tan, and his hair looked sun-bleached, and even though it was combed, it wasn't neat; it was slightly disheveled by the wind.

"Hello, what can you get... I... I mean, what can I get you?" Her face was now turning bright red, and she had no control over it.

"Well, I don't know; I have never eaten in a place this nice before. It would seem kind of odd just to have a beer, wouldn't it?"

"No, not really; we get all kinds of people in here that just want a beer and a cheeseburger. But you seem to be here to treat yourself, right? How much are you willing to treat yourself?"

"I don't do this often, so I want to do it right. What would you pick?"

"Are you allergic to seafood?"

"Nope."

"I know just what to get you."

She returned not too long after with a tumbler containing an amber liquid and a couple of cubes of ice.

"This is bourbon, top-shelf bourbon; your dinner will be out in a while. My name is Allison, by the way."

"Thank you, my name is Mitchell."

Mitchell watched her walk away; he was surprised at himself for being able to play it so cool. She was alluring and captivating; he didn't want her to leave but knew she had work to do. This was supposed to be a reward to himself for a long, hard work week, but now there was a purpose, a mission of sorts. What was his next step? He had to be smart about this; he knew she probably had guys hitting on her all the time, and she could already be seeing someone.

He put his thoughts in order; he would continue to flirt a little, just subtle enough for her to know he was interested but not enough to be overly obvious. Then, when he left, he would put the ball in her court.

Allison returned in a while carrying his plate; the smell of the dish was intoxicating and made his mouth water "Here you go. These are scallops cooked in the same bourbon you are drinking; that should give them more flavor. On the side is asparagus glazed with a butter sauce. Normally the portions are a little smaller, but I had the chef add a few extra for you. Want me to top off your drink?"

"Yes, please, but not too much; I do have to drive home."

He took small, slow bites, savoring every molecule. She was right; the bourbon he was drinking did bring out the flavor of the bourbon in the scallops and the scallops themselves. She recommended the blueberry cheesecake for dessert, which was just as delicious as the rest of the food. She asked if there was anything else he needed, and he politely asked for the check, all while his own tensions were building.

Allison had already told herself if this guy made a move, she would go for it. Not only was he handsome, but he was polite and kind as well. She could see he was interested but didn't try to monopolize her time; at least she thought he was interested.

She brought him the check and lingered for a little while, waiting for him to say something. But he didn't. Did she read him wrong? Did he not find her attractive? Had she played this all wrong? She left the table, fully disappointed, almost mad. She could tell by their facial expressions that the other waitresses could see the disappointment on her face. She was about to tell them she didn't care, as she needed to focus on her acting career anyway.

One of her friends happened to look over her shoulder and start smiling. She turned around to see what she was looking at, and there was Mitchell.

"Hey, what time do you get out of here?"

"Damn," she thought to herself, "why did I take a double shift today?"

"I am stuck here until ten," she responded.

"No, you are not. I will take your double, and you can take mine the next time someone like him walks in," one of the other waitresses said.

Mitchell blushed a little.

"Well, I guess I am off in about an hour, but you have to run me home so I can change."

"Deal."

A little more than an hour later, Mitchell was sitting in his truck outside of her apartment, waiting for her to come out. It had been fifteen minutes... nope, twenty minutes since she went inside.

The ride to her apartment was filled with small talk, the kind of noncommittal conversation that happens between two strangers who want to talk but don't know what to talk about. It was almost a half hour before she came out.

The dirty blonde hair that was up in a ponytail earlier was now down and brushed out. It looked like flowing water the way it curved around her face; it was what everyone was calling the Farrah Fawcett look, but she looked better than the Charlie's Angel to him. When she jumped into his truck, the smell of her shampoo and perfume blended in a bouquet of freshness that he breathed in and almost didn't want to exhale.

"So, what do you want to do?" Allison asked.

Now he was brought back to reality; he had sat in the truck for twenty-five minutes and hadn't given any thought to what to do next. He knew he didn't want to go to a movie; it was a nice, warm evening, and he wanted to be able to talk.

"How about mini golf?" he asked

Allison had put on her tightest jeans and wasn't too sure about walking around in them. She thought he would pick a movie; that's what everyone did. "Should I see if I can go change again?" she wondered. No, he had been patient enough; she would tolerate the tight pants for now.

"Mini golf sounds good. Do you know where there is one?"

"Actually, no, um..."

"I pass one on the bus to work every day; I will tell you how to get there."

Mitchell took the directions, and soon they were parked at the mini golf course. Mitchell had a hard time concentrating, as Allison's pants left little to the imagination. Her yellow top was one of those that was made to look like a button-up shirt but was tied up in the front, showing just a little midriff. Her skin was as tanned as his own; he got his from working in the sun, and she probably went to the beach when she had the time. Her shoes, or were they sandals... he didn't know; they were brown leather and open, and the soles looked like they were two inches thick.

Mitchell could have passed as a movie star, Allison thought, if not for his humble nature. He was obviously brought up with manners; he opened the door for her, always allowing her to go first, but this didn't just stop with her; he was kind to everyone. Then there were his looks; he didn't just look nice, but he dressed nicely too. He was wearing the popular bell-bottom jeans and a dark paisley shirt. He let his hair rest where it wanted to; sometimes it seemed to wave at her, beckoning to her.

He had his truck, so he had his own transportation; he had an apartment to himself that he had talked about, and he had a steady job. Mitchell wouldn't be a hold-up in her mission to become an actress. No, dating him wouldn't slow or stop that, she was sure.

ALLISON HAD PLAYED MINI GOLF a lot; it was something that she and her roommates would do when they had money left over after paying their bills. But she wanted Mitchell to put his hands on her. She wanted to feel his grasp and maybe start some playful touching. So, she placed her ball down and tried to stand as awkwardly as possible, with her feet close together and her hand backward on the club.

Mitchell hadn't played much mini golf, but he could tell Allison wasn't standing right. He also thought that Allison must come here a lot, as not only did she know just where this place was, but he had noticed a picture of her on the bulletin board in the office in the top player section. He knew just what she was trying to do and decided to play along. Why not?

"Hold on there and let me help you out." He stood behind her but left a respectful gap between them. He then took his hands over hers, covering them completely. He moved her hands to the correct positions.

"Now slide your feet apart a little." He now had his hands on her hips; she could feel his rough and calloused hands on her exposed skin. It sent a quiver up her spine.

She kept up the act for the entire game, letting him win. The evening was going well; it felt electric, and there was certainly a chemistry between her and Mitchell. After mini golf, they got ice cream and were eating it on the tailgate of his truck, both not wanting the night to end and both curious how it would end.

"If I ask her to come to my place, I could completely blow it," Mitchell thought to himself. "How can I ask her to come and make it sound like there are no... expectations?"

Allison was waiting for every touch, every physical interaction, like a child waiting for candy. Would he wait for the end of the date to try to kiss her? She ate her ice cream as slowly as possible, not wanting the end of the date to come.

Mitchell had eaten his ice cream so fast that he now had a headache; this didn't help his thinking at all. He figured if he finished his ice cream, that would make it easier to try to kiss her, but every time he thought he had a chance, she would be eating more of hers. She was taking her time with it for sure. Did she know he wanted to kiss her, and was she trying to avoid it? Maybe then he would just take her back to her place. She had talked a lot about trying to be an actress, and to him she seemed very focused and driven. Maybe she didn't want a boyfriend to slow her down. He respected that, which only made him more interested in her.

There were only a couple of spoonfuls of her strawberry ice cream left, and this date would, maybe, be over. Allison had tried to stall as much as she could, but the end was obviously coming. He wasn't even paying attention anymore. He was staring off with his head turned the other way. She decided to toss her dish; the trash can was right next to him, so she leaned a little in his direction to give the dish a toss.

Mitchell decided to turn back to her; it was rude to have his head turned away, and he didn't even realize he had done it. He had zoned out in thought. He would turn to her and help her down off the tailgate of his truck, and that would be that. Maybe they would exchange numbers, but he doubted it.

Allison and Mitchell both turned in each other's direction, both with a plan of movements that didn't involve their lips touching. But in a sweet and perfect accident, almost as if fate had intervened and pushed their heads together, their lips touched. Both had no intention of stopping once it happened. They stayed there, taking in each other and the random moment that brought them to where they both wanted to be.

The kiss built upon itself, much like an avalanche, and slowly faded much the same way. When their lips separated, both took a deep breath and smiled sheepishly at each other.

"Umm... well... ah." Mitchell stammered, failing to make sense.

Allison decided to throw caution to the wind. This had been the best night of her life since coming out here, and she didn't want it to end.

"Can we go back to your place?"

"Yes, yes, we can."

Mitchell helped her down off the tailgate and opened the door for her. He almost ran into the tailgate on his way back around the truck to get in. When he jumped up inside, he found that she was sitting in the middle now, whereas before she was on the passenger side.

The ride back to his apartment was filled with kissing, necking, touching, and caressing. Tension was building up, much like a kettle on the stove. Once in his driveway, they made their way up the stairs to his apartment, intertwined with each other.

The next morning, Allison reached over to hold her new lover, but there was no one on the other side of the bed. Her heart sank until her nose and ears sent messages that she was not alone in the apartment. She could hear sizzling sounds coming from the kitchen along with smells that were wafting from that area.

Not only had Mitchell woken up and started making breakfast, but he was also gentleman enough to take the covers that had ended up on the floor and gently cover her back up.

He saw Allison stir in the bed; she was awake. Would she freak out at the fact they had slept together? He watched as she sat up, holding a sheet to her bosom. She looked to the kitchen to see him standing there, watching her but not watching her. She didn't know what to say; it was such an awkward moment. She cleared her throat to get his attention.

"So... are we a thing now?"

IN A FEW MONTHS ALLISON had moved out of the apartment with the girls and had moved into Mitchell's apartment. This was both a good and bad thing. Mitchell's apartment was cheaper, and he would let her borrow his truck to get to work, though it was less than ideal for commuting in Los Angeles traffic. It was also a distance away from all her acting and singing lessons.

Mitchell could see that the situation was less than ideal for Allison, so he started looking for apartments closer to her work. He could manage the rent, but they wanted two months' rent and a security deposit up front. He called up his old boss, Steve Berger, and with his help, Mitchell was able to sell his parents' house. That would give them plenty of money and a little cushion. Next, he took his father's truck to a dealership and traded it for a Ford Escort station wagon; this would make much more sense for Allison to drive to work and to her classes. The last thing he did was pawn his dad's old shotgun; with that money and some from the sale of the house, he bought a ring.

They were out on a date, celebrating one year since they had started dating. It had gone by so fast, but Allison was an easy girl to love. The only flaw Mitchell saw was her obsession with becoming a star, and to him, he really didn't consider it a flaw. She was just driven and goal-oriented. Neither of them had a family, so why not dump everything into making her dream come true?

They were walking down Hollywood Boulevard, talking about the future and what they would do when Allison was finally discovered. Mitchell kept looking down, looking for the spot; they were close; it was 6901 Hollywood Boulevard. Then there it was, the star that represented Allison's favorite actress, the legendary Julie Andrews. Mitchell stopped and dropped to one knee while leading Allison in front of him. Over the star, he extended his hand with the diamond ring gripped tightly between his thumb and finger.

Allison was confused at first; she had been talking about the last audition she had been to, and when Mitchell went down, she figured he was going to tie his shoe. But when he guided her to stand in front of him, she looked down to see him kneeling just before Julie Andrews' star. Then came the ring. It was a little thing, but she knew he had sacrificed a lot to help her get her dream.

"Allison, I fell in love with you one year ago today. I love you with all that I am and all that we can be. Will you be my wife?"

"Yes."

CHAPTER THREE
The Fire

MITCHELL HAD JUST WIPED THE sweat from his brow; it had run into his eyes, and they were now stinging. Forty feet in the air was not a good place to start losing his vision. A couple of blinks and a wipe with a rag, and he was good to go. He picked up the yellow Bostitch framing nailer that started to feel like a cinder block. He had been coming in two hours early, working two hours later, and working on Saturdays. Allison was pregnant, and the baby was due in about a month.

Since becoming pregnant, Allison's personality had shifted; she changed. At first, he thought it was just the hormones that accompanied childbirth, but now it seemed she was angry. There was disappointment on her face when she told him she was pregnant, even a moment when he thought she was considering an abortion. Her biggest concern was that no one would hire her after having a baby. She often muttered something about her father, but when Mitchell asked, she would lash out.

Mitchell had no doubt that Allison would eventually get a role; he had already sacrificed so much to help her achieve that goal. He knew that one day she would land a role; she was good... no, she was great. But there were many girls out here with the same dream. So, Mitchell worked hard to give her every opportunity she could get, the best acting lessons, the best voice lessons; he completely invested in her success.

She worked too, as a waitress at a restaurant up until this month; it was a little hard to navigate through the tables with a beach ball on your stomach. They were in the home stretch now, one more month to go, and his baby girl would be welcomed into the world. They would be okay. He just had to keep moving, keep working, and stay positive.

"Hey, Mitch!" came a voice from below. He looked down to see the foreman. "Mitch, come down here; I got to talk to you."

Mitchell lowered himself down using the controls on the JLG boom lift. "What's up, Boss?"

"I am afraid the union is going to be shutting off your overtime."

"Boss... I am not union... you know that."

"Yeah, I know, but the union reps don't think it's fair that you are working an extra four hours a day when the other guys aren't."

"And let me guess, because the union has a cap on hours per week, they won't let them work extra hours like I do."

"You got it, Mitch!"

"Fuck, Boss... that cuts my paycheck in half!"

"I know, Mitch, but my hands are tied; I was supposed to put a stop to it yesterday, but I figured I would let you get a few more hours in, but today you need to clock out at 3:30 like everyone else."

Mitchell couldn't think of anything to say. He just turned and got back on his boom lift and went back to putting sheets of plywood on this mansion they were building.

At the end of the day, instead of getting a ride home, he decided to go to a bar that was just walking distance away. Some of the guys from the site would often go there, but he wasn't going to be social; nope, he wanted to clear his head and think. What better way to clear his head than a tumbler of whiskey? Just one, while he thought about how he was going to tell his pregnant wife that he had just lost half of their income. Just one, while he thought up plan B.

He sat down at the bar and met eyes with the bartender. Just some guy, about his age, probably trying to be an actor, just like his wife.

"What will it be?"

"Jack Daniels, neat, please."

The warm spirit was the last thing he needed; he knew he was dehydrated. A cold beer or gin and tonic would have been a better choice, but he needed to relax, and maybe he would ask for a glass of water when he was done with this. Another whiskey later, and anger started knocking at his door. He started stewing, thinking about how screwed up the situation was. He wasn't mad at the union members; they probably didn't care how much he worked. It was their representative that he was angry at; this was just a tactic to get more guys to join the union. Showing off their power so that people would sign up and feel protected. Then the door opened, just like it had been opening all along, but something told Mitchell to look over his shoulder to see who it was.

"Damn," said Mitchell in a raspy whisper.

It was the very last person that Mitchell wanted to see—the union rep who had just changed Mitchell's life. Mitchell decided it would be best to leave; if he stayed, things would go badly. He stood up slowly, making sure to be steady and not draw attention to himself. Then he felt a hand grasp his shoulder.

"Mr. Malcom, I hope there aren't any hard feelings towards us at the eight-five-five; we would love to have you sign up. We could even offer you a loan to help you through the financial adjustment."

Much like a forest fire starting, Mitchell Malcom's temper was starting to flare. The words "financial adjustment" was the ember. Mitchell Malcom turned around. His ice-blue eyes locked onto the vague, ignorant eyes of the union rep, who stood all of five feet tall of nothing and had a face so childlike it was almost prepubescent. Mitchell knew his temper was starting to build, but he still had control - if he could just maintain that control.

"Financial adjustment... you put me into this financial adjustment. Because you can't mind your own business, my income just got cut in half. My wife is eight months pregnant. I will have another mouth to feed, and now I have to do it with less, a lot less." He felt the ember building; it was best to stop before a fire started.

"Well, that's not my problem; I have to make sure that my union members are getting a fair deal. Now, I don't think it's very fair that you're doubling your paycheck and outworking my boys. This way, you will all be on the same playing field; nobody will be outshining anyone."

Tinder... Mitchell thought to himself, the ember had hit tinder and was starting to grow. Why didn't this guy just back off and walk away?

"Well, maybe if you union reps didn't try to control everything by putting caps on what people could work, some of the guys would pull some overtime. I know what you are doing. The cap slows progress, so you guys can milk out the contract and make the company pay you to lift the cap so we can meet the deadline. You guys get a sweet payout to divide amongst you reps, while you keep your thumbs on the very people you are supposed to be working for."

"Mr. Malcom... those are some lofty accusations. I hate to see you stir up trouble for yourself and your pregnant wife; what's her name, Allison? She is a peach."

Kindling... It's not what he said or how he said it. It was the fact that he even brought up his wife. This piece of garbage wasn't fit to breathe the air she breathed, much less utter her name. There was a wall right behind him. He could put him against that wall and scare the piss out of him. That would end this.

Mitchell placed his hand on the man's chest and pushed forward. The combination of being dehydrated, the whiskey, and the sudden rush of adrenaline didn't help when he tripped over the rep's foot as he was backpedaling. Mitchell started to fall and couldn't catch himself. All his momentum was focused on the hand in the middle of the rep's chest that was now sliding to his throat. Mitchell caught himself with his left arm, but most of his weight was now on his right hand at the rep's throat. The sound of the rep gasping for air echoed louder than any noise in the whole calamity. He felt himself being pulled off the rep, and just as he had his feet under him, a sharp pain from the top of his head traveled like a current to his spine, and then there was blackness.

Mitchell woke up to the sound of the armed guard saying his name. His head hurt; everything hurt. Wherever he was, there was no absence of light; it felt like needles burrowing into his eyes as he tried to open them. The walls were all white; as he gained more focus, he determined that the walls were cinderblocks, painted white. He looked around and saw a large picture window, but it wasn't to the outside. It was another room with people. People in brown uniforms with tan horizontal stripes. "Shit," he said out loud. He was in jail.

"No, no, no," he started saying out loud, as if by doing that it would rewind the events that put him here.

"Mr. Malcom, can you hear me?"

He looked in the direction of the voice and saw a man in uniform, holding a manila folder.

"Yes, officer," he said as he opened his eyes more as they adjusted to the light.

"Come with me, please."

When Mitchell put his feet down, he realized that he wasn't wearing shoes; they had been removed. A trivial thing, but a sure sign of just how much trouble he was in. He slipped on the jail-issued shower shoes and stood up. Then it occurred to him that he had no clue what time it was. He left the job site at 3:30, then two slow whiskeys; measuring time in drinks, that wasn't good. He didn't know how long he had been out.

"Officer... what time is it?"

"It is 9:07, Mr. Malcom."

"Oh shit... sorry, I don't mean to be disrespectful; I need to call my wife. I am usually home by now."

"Mr. Malcom, your wife has been notified where you are and is here in the waiting room. You are on your way to see the magistrate. The magistrate will determine if you are fit to leave or if you need to go back into holding until your trial."

"Trial?"

"Yes, for aggravated assault."

"Aggravated assault! All I did was push him a little and trip. What about who or what hit me?"

"Witnesses stated you tried to strangle the victim to the point he was heard gasping for air, and you didn't immediately get off him after falling to the ground. Witnesses said you had to be removed from the victim, and you still seemed hostile; the bartender struck you with a small wooden bat he had behind the counter."

Mitchell regretted ever going into the bar; he regretted ordering the first drink, the second drink, and ever putting a hand on that rep. The whole situation had spun out of control and proportion.

"Mr. Malcom, I need you to turn around and put your hands behind your back. I will be placing you in handcuffs while I walk down the hall to the magistrate and while we talk with the magistrate."

Mitchell slowly turned around, and then he felt the cold steel on his wrists. This officer wasn't taking any chances; he had the cuffs on tight. Mitchell couldn't blame him; the scene the witnesses described was not a good one.

The walk to the magistrate's office was just down the hall, but the hall seemed never-ending, like it just kept continuing on and on. Then the officer stopped and opened the door.

"This is Officer Jacobs with Mr. Malcom."

"Come in, please," said a voice from behind the door.

The officer opened the door and motioned for Mitchell to step in. It was a small compartment with reinforced glass separating him from the magistrate. On her side of the office was a large room with a large oak desk that was pushed all the way to the glass. The officer passed the manila folder through the mail slot to the magistrate. The magistrate opened the folder, and Mitchell could then see its contents. His driver's license was clipped to one side. She looked at it, then back at him, staring over the top of her glasses. The next sheet had the charges; she read them out loud. He wasn't sure if this was part of the procedure or if she just liked to do it that way. The next several pages were the witness statements. The room seemed to change its feel in a way Mitchell couldn't describe other than that time just seemed to slow down. She was reading what strangers perceived; he was being judged before he could say a thing.

"Ma'am, this was an accident; I..."

"Shoooosh," she interrupted. "You will get your turn, and when you address me, you better say 'your honor'; I have earned it.

"But you are reading the other side of the story first!"

"Yes, I am; then I will ask you for your side of the story. From there, I will choose whether to let you walk out of here, or not. If not, I will set your bail. I suggest you show some respect for me and the State of California."

Mitchell wanted to argue more, but he could tell that the officer had become tense.

"Yes, your honor."

She turned to the last witness statement page, and he found himself looking at the rep's neck, bruised with obvious finger impressions; the magistrate made a disapproving moan. The next sheet was the examination from the emergency room. She lifted that up so he couldn't see it. She placed all the paperwork back into the folder and looked up at him, peering over the top of her glasses again.

"Mr. Malcom, you are screwed." That's not what she said, but it is what Mitchell was thinking; what she really said was, "Mr. Malcom, what is your side of the story?"

Mitchell took a deep breath that actually felt refreshing given the air conditioning. He then started right from the beginning, right from finding out about the overtime until the sharp pain to his head that had knocked him out. Her face never moved, never changed, never faltered.

"Mr. Malcom, despite your lack of a criminal history, you have displayed that you have a temper and a lack of respect for your fellow human beings and the law. I am recommending you stay in custody until your court date one month from now and setting bail at ten thousand dollars."

"Ten thousand dollars! I don't have that kind of money!"

"A bondsman can bail you out; they usually ask for ten percent." She turned to the officer. "Take him away."

The next hour, all he could do was stare at the cell floor. What had he done? Another officer came in and said his bail had been posted. After getting his personal effects back, he was escorted out into a lobby. His wife was standing there, her face red and puffy from crying. She must have been so uncomfortable sitting in one of those folding chairs while pregnant, and nobody offered her a pillow or a cushion.

He opened his mouth to apologize.

"Shut up and get into the car," she said.

The next three weeks until his court date were the worst three weeks of his life. When he went back to work on Monday, he learned he had been fired. His boss did line him up with some under-the-table work. It paid well, but they were still burning through their savings. While walking home one evening, he walked by a Navy recruiter. He was twenty-five years old and in good shape; why not?

He told the recruiter about the pending court case. The recruiter told him that would be ok; he knew some people that might be able to help him out if he signed up. Mitchell didn't mention being married; he wasn't going to tell his wife. She would just talk him out of it. He would send her checks to take care of her and the baby. Mitchell had left her all the money he had; he sold off all his tools, personal items, and anything he had, even pawning his wedding band. He took all the cash, stuffed it in an envelope that he placed on the kitchen table; no note, no goodbye.

Mitchell Malcom got on a bus headed for the Naval Training Center in Great Lakes, Illinois.

CHAPTER FOUR
Melissa and the Director

AFTER MITCHELL LEFT, ALLISON GREW more spiteful and angry at the situation he had put her in; she decided to change her last name. To take it a step further she didn't change back to her maiden name of Cooligan. She chose a name that would sound good on a movie cover. Allison Malcom had died when Mitchell Malcom walked out of her life; now Allison Andrews would be the name people would see in movie theaters.

One week later, she lay in a hospital bed in pain, so much pain, and with the lack of insurance, they would not give her an epidural. Every time she closed her eyes to push, she hoped to open them and see Mitchell standing there. But he had ditched her; he ditched her when times got tough. Now, she was going through a tough time. Mitchell had left her all the money he had; he sold off all his tools, personal items, and anything he had and left an envelope with all the cash on the kitchen table. No note, no goodbye; she guessed he pawned his wedding band as well.

The real insult was she didn't even want a child; she had gotten pregnant by accident, and Mitchell insisted on keeping it. She knew having a baby would ruin any chances of landing any major roles. Mitchell tried to remind her there were plenty of actresses with kids, but she knew they had started their careers before having children. So now Mitchell, the one who actually wanted the child, was gone, and she was lying here in pain giving birth to it.

One more deep breath followed by a big push, and the baby was out. The doctor awkwardly looked for a father in the room to cut the cord, but the head nurse gave a subtle shaking of her head; the doctor took the hint and cut the cord.

"Ms. Andrews, you have a beautiful baby girl," announced the doctor.

The head nurse placed the baby in her mother's arms. Allison held the baby coolly, not so coolly as to show complete hatred but not as warmly as a new mother would.

"Oh, Melissa, what am I going to do with you?" she whispered to her newborn child. She had chosen Melissa as randomly as someone would choose what to have for dinner and with less care than someone naming a pet.

Shortly after being released from the hospital, Allison realized that to make whatever Mitchell left her in savings and in cash last, she would have to move out of the apartment, but she didn't want to move away from the Hollywood scene. She decided to live in her car, the one that Mitchell had bought her. Here she was, an aspiring actress, living in the back of a station wagon with an infant. All of her dreams had fallen; what would her father think?

Mitchell Malcom was a natural for the U.S. Navy. He was lean, strong, and had stamina. Being in shape going into bootcamp gave him a solid advantage, and along with already being in his twenties, it gave him a little more maturity over these... kids that had just graduated from high school. He had signed up as an E-2, Seaman's Apprentice, and advanced to E-3 Seaman while in bootcamp due to his behavior and leadership.

His goal was to make rate and advance as fast as possible and send all his money back to Allison. When he had heard about the extra pay allowances that the Navy SEALS got, he signed up to try out. After completing the six-month SEAL training in Coronado, California, he was assigned to SEAL Team 4, based in Little Creek, Virginia. Their area of concentration was Central and South America.

By this time, his mail had finally caught up with him. All the checks he had been sending to Allison had been returned, the envelopes stamped, indicating it was the wrong address. He tried to track Allison down; he even had his commander pull some strings. Nobody could find an Allison Malcom or an Allison Cooligan. She had disappeared along with his daughter. For the following years, he took the bare minimum of his paycheck for himself; the rest he saved for the day he would find his wife and daughter.

As time passed, Allison's situation didn't improve; she continued to live in the car, often seeking refuge at a friend's house or at a YMCA. To her, the auditions were a priority, so she often would take Melissa into the auditions, maybe to score a few sympathy points.

Melissa, now eight years old, would help her mother go through her lines before auditions. It was the only time Melissa ever felt a connection with her mother, the only time her mother ever acknowledged her. They walked into a studio, and Allison had set Melissa down in the lobby. On her way back to the set, she had left the door open.

Marvin Appleton had been watching actors try to act all day. He had had enough and needed to take a step outside to get some fresh air. He walked through the set door and noticed a little girl talking to herself in the lobby. He shook it off and proceeded to go outside. While sitting on the curb, he couldn't help but recognize the words coming from the little girl's mouth. She was reciting the words from the script and doing it with such passion and sincerity. He stood back up and cracked the door open to get a better look and to hear better. The little girl was out of her chair now; she was pacing while talking and moving her arms, making gestures. The part she was acting was opposite of the part he was screening today, and she was nailing it; the only problem was the part was for a teenager, and she was just a little girl.

"Maybe we could rewrite it?" he asked himself out loud. Even if he couldn't, there were a couple of other movies coming out, and this little girl could fit the bill. He stepped back into the lobby quietly, but it didn't seem to matter. The girl was ignoring him and sticking to the script.

"Excuse me... excuse me, little girl." The girl turned and looked at him, and the moment was electric. She had the eyes, the smile, and the posture. He had forgotten the words he was going to say.

"Yes, sir?"

"Ah... can you sing?"

"Sure, what would you like me to sing?"

"You choose."

Melissa cleared her throat and started singing.

"How do I get through one night without you? If I had to live without you, what kind of life would that be?"

She continued confidently through the entire first verse and the chorus when Marvin stopped her. It wasn't the best he had heard, but there was some power there and some raw talent he could use.

"How do you know that song, sweetie?"

"My mom has me sing it when she is in the shower at the YMCA; it's how she knows I am still there."

"Well, sweetie, your mom will not be showering at the YMCA for much longer, and she has you to thank for that. Is she here?"

"Yes, she is auditioning; she is going to be a famous actress."

"Can you tell me her name, sweetie?"

"Nope, you are a stranger; I'm not supposed to give names to strangers."

"Okay, that is fair. If I get you another script to read and bring another person to listen to you, would that be ok?"

"Sure."

Allison was perplexed; the casting director didn't even get to watch her audition. He had walked out, and by the time he had come back, she and a couple of other women had read their lines. Even then he wasn't paying attention; he was too busy talking to other people.

When the last person auditioned, a young lady stood up and called out.

"Would the mother of the child in the lobby please stay; the rest of you can leave; we will be in touch."

Allison's stomach hit the floor. What did Melissa get into? What did she break? She thought to herself as the other women filed out. The casting director that had completely ignored her now walked up to her.

"Are you the girl's mother?"

"Yes...what did she do?"

"Well, she just got the role in the next movie we are putting together, that is, if it is alright with you?"

"What about me? Did I get the part?"

Shocked at the response, this was the second time today Marvin found himself speechless.

"I don't know yet, ma'am; I need to go back through and watch the recordings, but your daughter doesn't even need to audition. She has the part, and we are willing to pay her a stipend now if you sign the contract as her legal guardian and adviser.

"Uh... stipend... how much?"

"I would be willing to give her one week's wages, let's say two thousand dollars; I can even make this check out to you, as you probably don't have an account ready for her. We have a list of agents for you to choose from; you will want to interview them and see which one will have your daughter's best interests in mind. Here is my card, and that is my personal phone number. If you have any questions, don't be afraid to call me. Ma'am, this is just the start. Once this movie is filmed and in theaters, your daughter is going to be famous; her life and yours are about to change dramatically. Try to stay in your role as mother; she will need you."

Ever since that morning at the audition, Melissa's career started to take off. First, just minor roles, her name not showing up on movie covers or posters. But her screen presence and how she got onboard with her character started to get noticed. After three films, she was given a lead role, then another, and another. Melissa and her mother went from living in a car to an apartment, then to a house. Melissa's mother tried to get her own career started with no luck; she used Melissa to get minor roles in movies, often being no more than an extra in the background. She was supposed to be taking care of Melissa's schooling and other parental responsibilities, which she soon started paying other people to do. She started to drink more and more. Before long, she just stayed at their house and drank while Melissa's crew took care of Melissa. There was no mother-daughter relationship. No peaceful moments having her mother brush her hair or talk to her about womanhood. Maureen, the housekeeper, was there for Melissa during her growing up, often going far beyond the requirements of a typical housekeeper.

Even with Melissa's schedule and her career taking off in a whirlwind, she tried to involve her mother as much as possible, but her attempts at building a relationship were futile. The more Melissa tugged at her mother to be by her side, the more her mother pulled away. Melissa tried asking about her father, trying to get any details. If she could find out anything, she would hire a private investigator to find him. But pressing her mother for any details at all was a catalyst for one of her drunken fits.

One night, Melissa pressed a little too hard; it started with Melissa asking about her father again, but then Allison started blaming Melissa for everything. She told Melissa that her father left because he didn't want her. Allison kept going, lashing out about her career and that Melissa had ruined it. Like a kettle coming to a boil, Allison started throwing things at Melissa. Melissa barricaded herself in her bedroom; she thought about calling the police but didn't want to hurt her mother more than she already had. She called her agent for help. Melissa's mother had expended all her energy and passed out by the time her agent showed up. Her agent put Melissa in a hotel room for the night. The next morning, Melissa's agent had a lawyer for Melissa to talk to; the lawyer had emancipation paperwork with him at the agent's request.

The lawyer presented Allison with an ultimatum: either she would willingly sign the emancipation for Melissa, or they would press charges of child abuse, and a judge would grant the emancipation. If she signed it, Melissa would let her live in the house, and Melissa would take care of all costs and would even provide her mother with an allowance of sorts. If it went to a judge, it would be a different scenario. Melissa's mother signed the paperwork.

Melissa was now a fully independent sixteen-year-old girl —well, as independent as she could be with an agent and the demands of a Hollywood career.

CHAPTER FIVE
Mitchell and Michael

MASTER CHIEF MITCHELL MALCOM WAS sitting at his desk, reflecting on his 16 years of service and thinking about what he had left behind, when he heard a knock on his door. "Come in," he barked. The door swung open, and a tall, broad-shouldered man wearing a Navy dress white uniform stepped into his office.

"What the fuck are you? You look like some type of highly decorated polar bear, son. Let me stand up and take a look at you."

Master Chief Malcom stood up from his chair and inspected the sailor before him. He knew he was getting his new boat driver, but that wasn't supposed to be until tomorrow.

"EN2 Williams, you're not supposed to be here until tomorrow."

"Master Chief, in my Navy, if you are early, you are on time; if you are on time, you are late, Master Chief."

"For fuck's sake, Williams, calm down. You are already here; that means I am already impressed. You are from Maine, right? You have been driving and working on boats since you were a toddler, right?"

"Yes, Master Chief."

Just then another sailor flew through the door. "Master Chief, we have a problem. BM2 Watts was supposed to be doing the security for Ms. Watson tonight, but he just came back from medical with a light duty chit. I need to find someone weapons qualled to be Ms. Watson's security for her time on base."

Master Chief Malcom pulled the service record from EN2 Williams' hand and opened it up to verify his weapons qualifications.

"QM3, I believe we have a solution right here; the early bird gets the worm, as they say. EN2 Williams, do you have your camouflage uniform available?"

"Yes, Master Chief."

"Would you mind changing into it, arming up, and being personal security for Ms. Watson? Ms. Jane Watson, the country singer, is doing a free concert on base tonight and tomorrow night. Think you can handle that until we get you assigned to a boat?" Malcolm loved giving orders in the form of a question; nobody ever said no.

"Yes, Master Chief."

"Go with QM3 here, and he will get you all the details. QM3, take him to the armory; if they have an issue, have them call me; copy that."

"Yes, Master Chief."

After getting the express check-in from QM3, Michael changed into his camouflage uniform, strapped on his gun belt, and signed out a vehicle from the motor pool. "Wow," he thought to himself, "I haven't been here an hour, and I am already armed and on an assignment." He knew the SEALS didn't mess around; they didn't believe in settling in. He wasn't a SEAL himself; he was assigned to S.W.C.C. (Special Warfare Combat Crewman), also called a "Swick." His job was to maintain and drive the boats to deliver SEALS and to cover their exit points. He was told about "special details," like his current assignment, when not deployed somewhere.

Jane Watson was a country sensation; she had recently won a CMA award and was shooting for female artist of the year. Michael approached her motorcoach and knocked on the door.

"Ms. Watson, I'm Petty Officer Second Class Williams. I am your security while you are here. I will be stationed out here by your door."

He turned and assumed the parade rest position. It was only a moment before the door to the coach opened. Williams turned slightly to see who was coming out. First, he saw the high-heeled black leather cowgirl boots with the "JW" logo in emeralds; those were followed by long, slender legs coated in tight denim, topped with a shiny belt buckle also with the "JW" logo. She showed a band of tanned midriff garnished with a small belly button piercing. A red and black flannel tied up, but not too high, covered a white sports bra. Her fiery red hair flowed over her shoulders like a waterfall. She swung her hair over her right shoulder, exposing a tanned face with green eyes. "What was all that? Petty what? Second who?" came her voice; if warm caramel had a sound, it was her voice.

"Uh, Petty Off... Just call me Williams, ma'am."

"Well, Williams, why don't you come inside? I can't have the press reporting that I left a sailor outside on a hot day."

Michael hesitated, but only briefly; he wasn't sure if he was supposed to go in, but they hadn't told him not to.

"Yes, ma'am."

"What will it take for you to call me Jane? Do I call the President, the Pentagon, or what?"

"No, ma'... no Jane."

It was an hour before Jane had to go on stage; in that hour, she and Williams talked and got to know each other. When it was time, he followed her through the barricaded crowd while she greeted her fans, then stood to the side of the stage, scanning the audience. Every so often he would look at Jane, and she would catch his eye and give him a smile. She was halfway through her set when it started to rain.

"Well, folks, the way I see it, y'all don't get to go home when it rains, so neither will I!"

Jane kept singing the entire show even when the rain was steadily falling. After the last song, she came offstage. Williams could see she was soaked, and even in the Virginia summer air, she was slightly chilled. He removed his blouse top and draped it over her and walked her to her coach. He opened the door, led her in, and turned around to leave.

"Williams, where are you going?"

"I won't be far, Jane; I will be in my vehicle just outside, keeping an eye on things."

"But you are soaked?"

"I have a spare uniform in my bag."

"Well, go get it, and you can change in here."

She could see the wheels of thought spinning in his eyes. Debating what he should do.

"Look, you are soaked; changing in the backseat of a Chevy Tahoe is next to impossible with wet clothes. Go get your bag and come back in here. I will leave you a towel. I will be in my bathroom taking a shower."

Michael thought for a moment; she was right; changing his uniform in the back of the Chevy Tahoe he had signed out would be difficult. He wasn't given clear details on this assignment other than to keep an eye on Ms. Watson; he had to stay close by. He gave her a nod of approval, then headed out to get a new uniform. He came back in and changed clothes quickly. He was putting on his gun belt when she came out of the bathroom.

She was wrapped in the blouse top he had let her borrow. Under that, a white t-shirt and flannel pajama bottoms.

"I dried your top, but it felt so warm, and it's so cozy I couldn't help but put it on again. I am going to have a drink; would you like one?" as she grabbed a bottle of Jack Daniels from a cupboard.

"No, I am on duty."

"Williams... don't be such a stick in the mud. You have got to have some fun once in a while. Look at you; you look like you're about to clear an enemy compound or something. Don't you ever relax?"

"When I am not on duty, Jane, you are in my protection. Your safety is my job."

"Okay, I get it. In that case, how about a Coke?"

"Coke is fine; I will need the caffeine to stay awake."

"What do you mean?"

"After you go to bed, I will stand watch outside."

"No, you won't; that is ridiculous; this coach has a security system, and the locks are heavy-duty. You can sleep in here with me tonight."

"What?!"

"You know what I mean, not with me but inside the coach. You can sleep on the couch."

He thought about it; strategically, it did make sense, not to mention he was supposed to escort her around tomorrow.

"You win again; I do need to check in in the morning; after that, I am supposed to take you to the hospital to visit wounded service members; then I believe you asked to go to the firing range, then a Black Hawk flight over the base and surrounding areas, correct?"

"Yes, then back here to prep for the second concert. After the concert, I roll out of here, and you will be rid of me." She said while passing him a maroon can.

"Dr. Pepper... I thought you said Coke?!"

"I am a southerner, sweetie; we call it all Coke. What do you call it? Pop?"

"Nope, pop is more Midwest; in New England we call it soda."

"Ah yes, I should have known by the accent. Williams, may I ask what your first name is?"

"Michael."

"Oohh, I like that, Mike."

Michael was going to correct her; nobody ever called him Mike. His mother hated people shortening his name. He chose not to; he really liked Jane. She took a seat next to him as they continued to talk. As they kept getting closer and the conversation changed tones, she stood up and turned on some music; it was one of her songs.

"Mike, will you dance with me... please?"

He was dead set on saying no until she paused and said please. He decided to take off the gun belt and his blouse top; it was getting a bit warm. He placed his left hand in hers, then placed his right hand on her side, just above her hip.

"Hmmm, a gentleman, I wouldn't expect any less. I never get to dance to my own music."

Michael had left a gap between them, but he was so regretting it now. His guard was fading along with his military bearing. He wanted to pull her in close and feel her body next to his. He had been single for a while and hadn't felt a woman's soft touch in a while. Her hand felt like silk in his. He closed his eyes, partly to steel himself and maintain some restraint but partly to savor the moment, to download it into his memory banks so he might relive it again in the future. In his thought process, he hadn't noticed she had stopped swaying. He opened his eyes only to be looking into her emerald-green ones. It took half a breath for him to react; he bent down and kissed her softly on her lips. Both his hands now were on her hips while she folded hers around his neck. He could feel the tip of her nose gently caressing his.

He took a step back, shocked at what he had just done.

"I am sorry; that was unprofessional," he said.

"Don't apologize; that was amazing; I am still tingling."

"I shouldn't have done that; I am on duty, and you are my principal."

"Principal... I am a woman, a woman that finds you attractive. You are a man—a man that finds me attractive. We are in the safety of my coach. Your job is done for the night. In the morning you can go back to being a soldier boy, but for now, be Mike, be with me."

He needed a moment, a pause, a time-out to think. He walked to the bathroom and closed the door. He looked in the mirror. This command was an opportunity of a lifetime, and Master Chief Malcom had a reputation for building sailors. Why risk that? What risk was there? So, what if he kissed her? It was done, over with. He would go back out, they would talk some more, then she would sleep in her bed, and he would sleep on her couch. He opened the bathroom door, ready to follow his plan, until he looked to find her wearing his blouse top; only his blouse top, and not a single button was fastened.

Michael woke the next morning in her bed; she was out in the kitchen area making breakfast, still wearing his blouse top but with her pajamas underneath. Before he could reflect on last night, he heard her speak to him.

"Get outta bed; we got stuff to do. You need to check in with your boss, and I need to get ready to go to the hospital. When you talk to your boss, can you see about me going to the beach? I think there is time between the hospital and the Black Hawk ride."

The day seemed surreal to Michael and almost confusing; at the hospital, he escorted her around to the wounded servicemen and women; she stayed a distance from him; he avoided any cameras, leaving that moment to the wounded. Every so often she would give him a wink, though; that would jog his memory of the night before. They returned to her coach and eventually changed into beach clothes, and he drove her to Virginia Beach in his personal vehicle to maintain a cover.

While at the beach, Jane bought a baseball hat and some larger sunglasses to help cover more of her face. She was wearing a pink bikini under a white tank top and cutoff blue jeans. Michael bought her a hot dog, and they shared fried dough from one of the local shops. After eating, they took a swim in the water and roughhoused, splashing each other. Michael could lift her up so easily. After swimming, they lay on towels, talking.

"So, Petty Officer Michael Williams, what is in your future? What is your big plan?"

"I want to stay in the Navy until I retire. I may try out for the SEALS; I like being at the sharp point of the sword. Sneaking in, sneaking out, no sign that we were there other than your objective."

"No plans for a wife or kids?"

"We will see; right now, I want to serve my country. If I meet a woman worth marrying... I don't know. I don't like to half-ass anything, and it would be hard to be a good husband or father while giving my one hundred percent to the Navy. What about you? Other than your music career, what are your dreams?"

"I just want to have fun. I don't care where I am going or what I am doing. I just want to have fun while I am doing it... or him," Jane said while giving Michael a poke.

After the beach, they returned to her coach and showered together. Then it was off to the Black Hawk helicopter flight. For him, the real fun on the Black Hawk ride was her smile; she had a huge grin the entire time, and when the pilot gave them a sudden drop, she grabbed for him for safety. The members of the crew noticed but made no comment.

They ordered pizza and ate together before she got ready to go back on stage to sing. As Michael walked her to the stage, he was trying to figure out what the next move was: could they pull off a long-distance relationship? It was worth a try.

While she was on stage, Michael tried to reason with himself about what he should do. He managed to separate the fact she was famous; all he had seen was a simple, fun-loving woman who didn't mind hanging out with someone... normal. He decided that he would ask to keep this going after she left Virginia. He wanted to give a relationship with her a try, and if it failed... so what? At least they would have some fun. If it worked out, well, he could always get out at the end of his enlistment and be her head of security. His heart started to feel warm at the thought, and pictures of flying to different concert locations started flashing in his head.

After the concert was over and, on the walk back to the coach, he planned out the conversation in his head. Then he noticed the light in the coach was on; someone was inside. He started to unholster his weapon while trying to get a step ahead of her. The coach door flew open, and out came Trent Dell, another country singer. He slowly put his sidearm back, and, in the meantime, Jane ran into Trent's open arms, jumping up and wrapping her legs and arms around him. Their lips were tied together while Trent held her up by her buttocks. He let her down and turned to Michael.

"Who is this guy?" Trent asked Jane.

"That's my security, Petty something Wilkins...Williams."

"Let's get inside and make up for the lost time; Wilkins, if the coach is a-rockin, don't come a-knockin."

He looked at Jane, who seemed to giggle at the rhyme. There was no apology or remorse in her eyes. He had been used and tossed aside. He was left with the pain of it allL. "Never again," he said through gritted teeth. "Never fuckin' again."

CHAPTER SIX
The Russian

OVER THE NEXT FEW YEARS, Michael made a home for himself with SEAL Team 4. The boats in Michael's care not only had the best maintenance records, but they were also the cleanest. Master Chief Malcom stated he could eat his Wheaties out of the bilges of one of Michael's boats. Michael had proved his mettle in battle too, always keeping the SEALS' exit path open. He was also one hell of a boat driver, even under fire. Today, Michael and Master Chief were at the firing range together. It was known among SEAL Team 4 that if Master Chief Malcom wanted to have a "talk" with you, you were going out to the pistol range.

"How do you feel about this mission coming up, Williams?"

"I feel good about it, Master Chief. I drive in, the team takes the baby ribs in, and I monitor the airwaves and the beach. If things get hot, I provide suppressive fire and keep the door open for them. No different than any other mission we have run."

"That is where you are wrong, son; no mission is like every other one. Williams, I need your head in the game. This is a big, bad Russian; we have no name on him, but the CIA has been tracing him. They won't even tell any other agency about him because he has people everywhere. This guy used his own wife as a human shield to not get caught."

"Yes, Master Chief, I understand; I am in it. You have nothing to worry about."

"I heard you are interested in stepping out of Swick and trying out for SEALS?"

"Yes, Master Chief, I have been hitting the gym and running extra. I have also been talking to the guys and learning what to expect. My plan was that as soon as I thought I was ready, I was going to come to you and submit the paperwork formally."

"I already think you are ready, and I have already put the paperwork in for you. You go to Coronado as soon as we get back from this next mission."

"Thank you, Master Chief; I won't let you down. Any advice?"

"I know you won't; you have the drive and the brains. I already told them I want you back here with me when you finish. As far as advice, embrace the suck. Now I hear you are a damn good shot with a pistol; you had a group the size of a basketball at 100 yards."

"That is right, Master Chief; I go to the range twice a week."

"Don't forget to give yourself a personal life; you can't be 'Go Navy' all the time."

"Master Chief, I see the guys with families here, and nothing against them, but when I start a family, I don't want them worrying about me on some mission. I want to be there for everything."

"I can understand that; it will also help you keep your focus. You know what, Williams? I may be jinxing you, but I think you've got what it takes to be a SEAL. I usually wait for people to graduate BUDS before I give them this, but just in the off chance you don't come back to this team, I will give you mine."

Master Chief Malcom rolled up his sleeve, and Michael could see him removing some Velcro straps. He had heard about these spring-loaded knives that the Master Chief's team wore on their wrists. They were not regulation by any means, but the Master Chief said they could come in handy someday.

"Williams, all you have to do is adjust the pull string and put the ring on your finger. When you jerk your hand up, the ring pulls the string, and the string releases the blade. It has enough force to pierce clothing and skin, and the blade will make short work of zip ties if you were ever bound," Mitchell said as he passed the wristband knife to Michael.

"Thank you, Master Chief."

Master Chief Malcom was a SEAL, no different than others. He was laid-back but not soft. He had much concern for the SEALS with families. He wouldn't reschedule an op, but he would change training schedules so one of his guys could make it to a son's ball game or a daughter's dance recital. He was in full contact with the SEALS' wives' club and even authorized some of the more serious girlfriends to be members. He also scheduled family days for the SEALS and their families to meet; they went to baseball games and cookouts; he knew every wife's and girlfriend's name and their kids' names. He even played Santa Claus at the Christmas party. It was rumored that someone once asked why he wasn't married; the Master Chief changed the subject quickly and coldly. He did once let it slip, while drinking after an op had gone bad and they lost a SEAL, that he didn't deserve a family. Everyone thought that was because of the guilt he felt because he had lost a man.

A couple of days later, in the well deck of the USS Oak Hill, Michael was waiting for the ship to flood the well deck so he could get floating. As soon as the water was up to the hull, he started the engines. The two Yanmar diesels came to life. The thirty-three-foot jet-driven boats were perfect for river combat. This boat was an SOC-R and was built specifically for river patrols. It had a total of five different machine guns and two grenade launchers. Each man had an assault rifle on him and a sidearm as well. Each boat carried three Swick members (two gunmen and one helmsman) and four SEAL members (two of the SEALS would man guns). Three boats were going in up the river, and then the SEALS would get into little electric-propelled inflatable dinghies, or baby ribs, as they called them. There was a meeting going on between the Russian and some cartel members. The SEALS would go in, grab the Russian, collect any intel, and then leave the same way they came in. The secondary exit plan was helicopters. If they went to secondary, it would be up to Michael and the Swick crews to get out of the river and back to the USS Oak Hill.

It was the perfect night for an op; no moon, and low-lying fog was infiltrating the shoreline. Michael was sure that fog would be covering the river. He had night vision goggles and had the course mapped out on the GPS unit. The boats pulled out of the well deck of the ship and sped for the coastline. Master Chief was in Michael's boat, so he had the lead. Word was Master Chief requested to be on Michael's boat. He wasn't sure if that was a sign of confidence or if it was that Master Chief wanted to keep an eye on him.

Michael scanned the coastline as he entered the river; there was nothing, not even on radar. He opened up the range on the radar and still saw nothing for miles. He made the call on his comm set that he was "leaving his radar wide," meaning he was going to leave the range at max. This would take the sensitivity down but give him a wider view. The other two boats would keep their radar narrow and focused on the immediate area. This wasn't part of the mission brief, but the Master Chief gave him a nod of approval.

They were in the river now; Michael cleared his head and focused on his driving. Master Chief was standing beside him, watching the radar and the GPS so Michael could concentrate on the river. They were at eighty percent throttle, a little over thirty miles per hour, saving the other twenty percent of throttle for an emergency. A few days before, the DOD had flown a small stealth drone through here; Michael and the other helmsmen watched the video until it was memorized. Soon they were at the drop-point. Michael assisted in getting the baby rib off his boat. He engaged the skyhook, a navigation feature that would allow for the GPS to control the engines and steering to keep the boat within a meter of where it was set. Michael manned the fifty-caliber machine gun and kept a watchful eye. He watched the SEALS disappear into a smaller creek that fed into the river; every thirty heartbeats, he would look at the radar and ask for a radar check from the others.

"Fuck!" Michael said under his breath as he looked at his radar. "Alpha One, this is Night Guard," Michael called to Master Chief using the prescribed code names.

"Go for Alpha One."

"Alpha One, I have a contact inbound to my location. It is fifty clicks out and will make contact in twenty minutes."

"Copy that, Night Guard; stay cold. It could just be a recon flight, and I don't want to spook anyone. We are at the target point now and about to…"

The explosion was so big Michael could feel some of the shockwave where he was; he looked to see a huge ball of fire going into the sky.

"Booby trap… sec…ond…ary…" was all Michael could make out on his com set. He couldn't even hear who said it.

"Repeat the last transmission." Michael said into his comset. He wanted to be sure they were using the secondary exfiltration plan before he left.

"Williams, let's go! They said secondary; you said there is a contact inbound," yelled one of the other helmsmen.

"Shut the fuck up and sit tight; I need to confirm the call to secondary." Michael regretted losing his cool momentarily. There was a long and eerie silence

Michael was about to try the com set again when he heard a familiar voice on his com set.

"Target booby-trapped, secondary exfil no good, SAM (surface-to-air missiles), and anti-aircraft guns. Night Guard, we are heading your way, primary exfil."

Michael looked at the radar; the contact would be closing in soon; it was following the river, probably sweeping it.

"Alpha One, this is Night Guard; I am taking one boat upriver to engage with inbound contact."

"This is Alpha One, I confirm; good luck."

Michael turned off the skyhook and started up the river at full throttle. He didn't know this part of the river; it wasn't on any of the footage he had studied; he had to be focused. If he could approach fast enough, he could hit them before they knew where he was. He was sure his boat would not show up on their radar. He couldn't look up into the sky himself; he had to focus on the river. He had to trust his gunners.

Whap, whap, whap, whap, whap.

His thoughts were interrupted by the sound of his gunners, who had seen the incoming contact, an older UH-1H, at the same time. They were rewarded with the sound of their rounds hitting the sheet metal of the fuselage. They must have hit the pilot because the helicopter flew erratically for a moment. The gunner in the helo was able to get a few shots off in their direction. Michael executed a one-eighty maneuver to send them back out of the river; in that moment, the gunner was able to get a fix and fire more shots at them before the helo went down. Michael could hear the shots ricocheting around him. He felt a terrible pain in his groin; the bulletproof glass had a crack with a bullet stuck in it, and it aligned with his head.

"Anyone hit?" Michael yelled to his crew members while wincing with his own pain that was getting overwhelming.

All his crew members answered back. He could breathe a little easier now, or could he? His eyes started blurring; the pain was overtaking him now. He reached down, and it felt warm and wet. He said "help" into his com set before passing out.

When he woke up, he was in the medical ward of the USS Oak Hill. He looked down to see his legs were spread apart. He tried to move so he could reach or see what had happened.

"Don't panic, Williams; you can still use the men's room. A ricochet caught you in your femoral artery; it just nicked it; otherwise, you would be dead. That is the good news. The bad news is it shattered your hipbone; it's a wonder you stayed vertical as long as you did."

"Any casualties, Master Chief?"

"Nope, some are a little banged up, but we got out of there. We sent a UGV in first; it set off the trigger. Somebody knew we were coming. Somebody who knew we would normally have our radar set at five clicks instead of fifty. Someone who knew about the secondary exfil plan. That fuckin' Russian has a long reach, or his boss does. The CIA has already heard him bragging about the information he got from someone named The Archer; they are starting a file on him."

Master Chief looked at Michael for a while. Michael could tell there was something else he wanted to say.

"What is it, Master Chief?

"Look, right now your hip bone is in pieces; the whole left side is shattered. The bullet that hit you had ricocheted off something, so it was like getting hit with a large musket ball. The docs on this ship did their best to get the artery fixed, but they can't do anything about the hipbone. Once we are back in Virginia, you will be going into surgery to replace half of your hip and the joint. So, you will be down and out for a while, then..."

"No SEALS..." Michael interrupted.

"No SEALS, no Navy, son. You will be medically discharged after you complete your therapy." Master Chief replied.

Michael noticed some of his gear off to the side. He reached for the wrist knife, but Master Chief put his hand on his shoulder.

"Williams, you keep that. You earned it tonight."

Every time Michael closed his eyes for the next few weeks, all he could see was that bullet stuck in the windshield of the boat. It was odd; that was bothering him more than getting his hip replaced. If that bullet had been just a few millimeters to the left, it would have hit his femoral artery, and he would have bled out. But that one bullet stuck in the glass that should have hit him in the head —that was what was haunting him.

The medical discharge was looming over Michael's head like a storm cloud. The last thing he wanted was to get out of the Navy; he considered serving his country a privilege. Now, he would be going back to Maine to work at a boatyard as a diesel mechanic, at least until he could start his own business. Master Chief had visited him a few times while he was in physical therapy, and he had made the decision to retire from the military and go to work for the CIA as an SSO (Special Skills Officer) so he could continue his pursuit of the Russian.

Before his retirement, Master Chief Mitchell Malcom and the rest of SEAL Team 4 gathered in his hospital room, all in their dress uniforms. Master Chief presented Michael with a small box. Michael opened it slowly to find he had received the Purple Heart award, the award given to those injured in combat. It was a bittersweet award; yes, it was nice, and it did show he had made a sacrifice, but all he did was get hit with a stray bullet—it wasn't like he jumped in front of it. He was thinking about what to say; with all these mixed feelings, it was hard to come up with a thought. Then Master Chief passed him another felt box. He opened it to see the

Bronze Star; everyone in the room popped to attention and saluted while Michael took it out of the box.

"Michael, it was your quick thinking and bravery that made it possible for all of us to be standing in this room; thank you." Master Chief said after clearing his salute.

CHAPTER SEVEN
Goodbye, Mother

Since breaking ties with her mother, Melissa became more involved with the business side of being an actress. Her agent helped coach her along with her image. Melissa would have been happy just to live in a small house, but her fame required something more secure and lavish to keep up with other actresses. She bought a mansion in Beverly Hills. The mansion was built the same year as her birth. All she knew of her father was that he worked in construction and was building a mansion in the area when he left her mother; maybe it was this one. Maybe in some weird way, she would have some type of parent sheltering her, if only indirectly. She had tried to find him but had little to go on, as his name wasn't on her birth certificate. Her mother certainly wouldn't tell her more now. All she could hope was that someday her father would see her on TV or in the movies and come forward if he was still alive.

HER AGENT ALSO DIRECTED HER social life, setting her up with dates for large events. Most often it was other teenage celebrities, but sometimes male celebrities in their twenties. Nothing ever crossed any line. Her agent would tell her it was to "pump up" the media. She found out that sometimes the other agents were actually paying her agent for their client to be seen with Melissa. She could trust her agent, though; she had been with her from the start, but it didn't help the feeling that she felt like a piece of meat being sold. None of the dates were real. Her first kiss was on set with a boy she didn't know. She envied the characters she often played; they had such vibrant social lives. Going to the movies, dancing, the prom. Her social life was very different. A tutor was part of her entourage, basically homeschooling her while at home or at whatever location she was filming. She really didn't even know what actual grade she was in and was further shocked when a diploma arrived by mail from the Beverly Hills school system. Apparently, she had done well, having a 3.8 GPA, but there would be no ceremony, no climactic finish, no parents hugging her, telling her they were proud of her.

Her twenties were much the same, except she found herself being cast in much more sexualized roles; she even looked back at some of her older teenage films and found that had started sooner than she had realized. The costumes became more revealing. She started to take a stand in that regard; she let her agent know there would be no nude scenes. She wanted to take back some of the control of her career again and wanted to be more of an actress than eye candy. She started focusing on the skills that got her to where she was; she started taking voice lessons and dance lessons again.

Melissa felt like she had a new momentum, a new fuel within her. She had also started dating a football star; this was her first real boyfriend. Colin had sought her out, giving her his number directly at a celebrity charity event. He was too shy to say anything or was worried about being overheard. He just placed the number in her hand while greeting her and walked away. She had waited a day before calling him, not sure on how to handle it, and she didn't feel like involving her agent either.

The first date was an adventure; she felt like a schoolgirl breaking out of the dormitory. He had told her to dress down —nothing fancy, low-profile. He picked her up in a small, compact rental car. He took her bowling—a first for her. Soon they started to attract attention, so they left and went to the movies. After the movie, he found a small diner for dinner. He dropped her off back at her mansion and gave her the first real kiss on the steps at her front door.

Their relationship grew from there; she had gone to watch some of his games, and he had come on set for her recent movie. The director even used him as an extra; an Easter egg like that would surely help promote the movie. Things got more serious and more intimate as they spent more time together.

One weekend, while she was filming in Dubai, she turned on the TV to see him kissing a model at a nightclub. She was crushed and broken, so much so that she had to take the next day off—something that was strange because she had a good reputation as a hard worker. One of her co-stars was concerned, so he went to visit her in her hotel room. That is how her friendship with Chris Pratt was forged.

For the first time in her life, she felt like she had a true friend with Chris—nothing sexual, no drama, just a true and solid friend. She could let down her guard and just relax and be herself.

While at home relaxing one afternoon, her housekeeper, Maureen, came into her living room.

"Ms. Andrews, there are police here; they will be knocking on the door shortly. I believe it would be best if you greeted them with me."

Melissa knew not to question this; it was an odd request from her housekeeper, and her housekeeper typically didn't make odd requests. Soon, just as she said, there was a knock on the door. Maureen opened the door and asked the police to come in. The two police awkwardly stepped inside, both hesitant to look Melissa in the face.

"Can I help you, officers?" Melissa asked, trying to prompt them a little.

The older of the two officers seemed to fortify himself a little and looked Melissa in the eyes.

"Ms. Andrews, this morning at around nine-thirty, your mother was found dead."

She knew she should feel something, that the pain should be more; it should be worse, but it felt no different to her than saying her car had been hit. In the long pause it took to respond, there was a level of guilt for not feeling hurt; that seemed to hurt even more.

"Where... where was she found?" Melissa stammered out.

The older officer shuffled his feet; the details were going to be hard to report.

"She was found on her front lawn. She was naked except for a sheet wrapped around her. She was holding a bottle of vodka."

Each individual word felt like a bee sting to her heart. She couldn't understand the blend of emotions that were swirling inside her. She found it hard to breathe; she was faltering. Then she felt the warm, supportive hand of her housekeeper. Maureen, who was always so stoic and professional, never showing any interest in Melissa other than keeping the estate running, had now stepped out of that role, if only for a second. Through that hand on her back, she drew strength to talk some more.

"Do I need to do anything?"

"Yes, you will have to come down to the city morgue and identify the body."

"Identify the body" echoed in her head as if the police officer had said it in a long and vacant hallway. She heard Maureen speak to the police, then she gently escorted them out. She directed Melissa to a chair.

Maureen knew what she was supposed to do was to contact Melissa's agent, but Maureen didn't trust her agent and knew she would turn this into a media circus in which Melissa would be the show. Maureen had learned a lot through the years working for these people; she had a few tricks up her sleeve. First, support: Melissa would need support when going to the morgue; she would go with her, and she would also call Chris Pratt. Next, a diversion; she needed to lead the paparazzi away from Melissa, making them think she was headed elsewhere. Quickly, all this had to be done quickly; she was sure someone either at the police station, morgue, or wherever would soon leak about the status of Melissa's mother and how she was found.

She contacted Chris, letting him know what had happened and what her plan was. She then called one of the local restaurants, one she knew had loose lips around the media, and said Melissa would be arriving shortly to meet a new boyfriend there. She then grabbed one of the gardener's spare straw hats and had Melissa put it on, along with jeans and a T-shirt. Maureen had a small Mercedes SUV that Melissa had provided her for transportation and running errands. The media knew of this SUV and dismissed it. They picked up Chris Pratt on the way and headed to the morgue.

The media hadn't found out yet. The city morgue was quiet. Melissa was able to walk in without issue. They led her to a body that was covered in a clean white sheet. The mortician looked up at Melissa, and she gave him a nod. He folded down the sheet. At first, it didn't look like her mother at all, like there had been a mistake. Then, features started to show. The alcohol had changed her face considerably since Melissa was sixteen, but the major features were there enough, and the longer Melissa looked, the more the stranger's face became the one she remembered. She remembered the last time she saw her mother alive, the awful things her mother said, and the things her mother had thrown at her while she fled to her bedroom. Melissa took off the straw hat just to lean on Chris. "Why couldn't she just love me?" she said, in almost a whisper.

Less than a week later, Melissa was giving a press conference, looking as strong as she could muster. She wanted to show her fans her strength and resolve—that she wasn't some frail starlet but a strong woman. She had her mother cremated and stored the urn away, out of sight, in her mansion. She had no clue what to do with it. She held no funeral or reception.

CHAPTER EIGHT
Melissa and her Agent

MELISSA ANDREWS SAT IN HER kitchen facing her agent with the latest movie script in her hand.

"What the hell? I trusted you. I signed that contract thinking that you had read through it. You told me it was good to go, so I signed it. Now I see there is a nude scene in the script. I told you I don't do nude scenes," yelled a furious Melissa Andrews to her agent.

"Melissa, more and more actresses are doing nude scenes. This is just a butt shot. Come on, college kids moon and flash each other all the time. Don't be such a prude," argued her agent.

"Listen, Janet, I don't care about what college kids do. If I start doing butt shots now, they will want more later. The way that scene is written, I am basically on set in the nude. You know how many people are on set. There are plenty of actresses that don't do nude scenes. Can't you get me a body double?

"Nope, not in the contract."

"Call the director or producer; see if they will budge a little."

"No way, Melissa, you will get the reputation of being hard to work with. Look, it's a couple of seconds. Someone will have a towel or bathrobe ready as soon as the scene is over."

Melissa stared at her kitchen floor. These days, it didn't seem that Janet, her agent, had her best interests at heart. What could she do? She had signed the contract. She would push back, though. Keep a towel on as long as she could, then drop it at the last minute. One take, that is all she would give them.

"Okay, but this is it. Never again, and we do it in one take."

"That is fine, but I don't understand why you are so uptight about this. You are gorgeous and have a beautiful body. You were Maxim Magazine's top ten."

"It's not that I am insecure; it's my body, and I only want to share it with people that I want to share it with. Also, it's not the message I want to send to my fans."

"Half of your fans are male; they will love it!"

"Not the kind of love I am looking for, Janet, and I don't want to delve into that subject."

"Okay, then, moving on, how soon do you want to get to Hawaii, and what arrangements do you want made?"

At this point, Melissa didn't even want to go to Hawaii anymore. She was already tired of this film, and she hadn't even started it yet. The producer was a known pervert, but she liked the story, the director was great, and she liked the rest of the cast. There were going to be some steamy kissing scenes that would push her boundaries a little. She would have to spend some time with her co-star to build up some rapport before filming even began.

Before that even happened, she wanted to start her process of becoming the character, Madison, a surfer, surf instructor, and waitress. Not only that, but Madison was vegetarian. So, she had to take surfing lessons, go undercover as a waitress, and stop eating meat. Madison lived in a small bungalow on the outskirts of town and lived a simple life. Melissa found a bit of irony in how close her story and her character's parallels were in some ways. Madison still had her father, a motorcycle mechanic, but he was so involved in work he might as well have been dead. Madison did have a little sister, whom she had been taking care of since they lost their mother at sea. Then you had Madison's boss at the resort, who was much like Melissa's producer, a downright pervert. Madison did have a boyfriend, a serious boyfriend.

The other thing Madison had that Melissa didn't was a hobby. Madison loved to surf, and surfed as much as she could. She would get up early to go surfing before the day started, often making her late for work, putting her in the crosshairs of her boss. There were other conflicts at play that would give the film more depth, not just a surfer movie or bikini frenzy.

"Earth to Melissa. Did you hear me? How soon do you want to get down there?"

"Let's get down there as soon as possible. I want to reach out to some of the cast myself, the girl who will be Madison's sister and the boyfriend, but I want to keep my distance from the father; I actually don't want to know who has that part. I think that would be best due to the tension and absence between her and her father."

"There you go; that's my Melissa Andrews, ready to get to work!"

Janet showed herself out of the mansion under the piercing eyes of Melissa's housekeeper, Maureen. Maureen hated her; she knew it; she could tell by the way Maureen looked at her and how she didn't call her first when Melissa's mother died. No matter, Janet had secured the "butt shot," as she called it. The producer would be giving her a little extra now. She needed it too.

Janet acquired a bit of gambling debt, hundreds of thousands, spread out from casinos, horse race brokers, and others. If word got out, she could lose her license to be an agent. She could simply ask Melissa for the money, and she would probably give it to her, but she didn't want Melissa to know about her problem. The producer knew; that's why he had offered her a... bonus for Melissa agreeing to do the nude scene. Hopefully, by the time she shot the scene, she would be more cooperative.

A few weeks later, Melissa had settled in a small, two-room bungalow that was a 20-minute drive from the resort that her character worked at and where much of the filming would take place. She was getting the basics of surfing down; she had a stunt double for any tricks or dangerous shots. She just needed to be able to look confident on the board and be able to get some good action shots. She did spend some off-time kayaking to get out on the water; oddly, she felt the ocean seemed to call to her.

Melissa, with help from her agent, had also gone undercover and gotten a job waitressing at a local restaurant. The owner didn't even know who she really was. At first, she found the job terribly difficult. Lots of time on her feet, writing down orders, remembering what table ordered what. She couldn't believe how rude some people could be and how some customers would treat her after a minor mistake. One of the other waitresses there saw Melissa struggling and lent a hand when she could, helping Melissa remember which table and how to "kill with kindness" when a customer was rude. She even gave Melissa some of her tip money and wouldn't take no for an answer.

She had invited the actress that was to play her sister over for sleepovers and even took her out on shopping trips. She and her co-star boyfriend set up a few staged dates. She knew that her co-star was married and went as far as meeting with his wife and taking them both out to dinner. She kept her distance from her "father" so that her scenes with him would be awkward and distant. For her "boss" in the movie, she just pictured the producer; they seemed to have the same qualities.

The film schedule was hard: lots of early morning shots of surfing and late nights of shooting the waitressing scenes. Then there were the love scenes that were always awkward, but Melissa handled all of it well. She enjoyed working with the younger actors, trying to pass on any tips and knowledge. The movie was going very well, and she felt like she was delivering the character well.

The day came for the "butt shot," as she called it. The scene was to be taken in one of the hotel rooms of the resort. Madison's boss has given her an ultimatum: either sleep with him or lose her job. The boss was waiting in the bedroom of the hotel suite. Madison is first shown from the neck up, her motions alluding to her undressing. The scene then shifts perspective as if the clothes she just tossed on the floor are watching her go into the room, showing her naked bottom as she walks into the bedroom.

Melissa studied the contract and the script heavily and decided to exploit every loophole or missing detail. The first thing she insisted on was that there were to be no cellphones on set. Nobody was to be able to take a picture at any part of the scene. Second, she chose a larger-than-normal bikini for the first part of the scene; this was to cover up a slightly smaller, flesh-colored bikini that the director, producer, and even her agent didn't know about. She had taped the front of the lower part of the flesh-colored bikini on. All they were going to get was her bottom, nothing else. With all this in place, she gave the scene her all.

Even with all her planning, the feeling of exposing just her bare bottom felt cheap and wrong; she didn't even wait for the director to say cut before grabbing a towel and covering up. The director was happy with the scene, the producer was furious, and her agent was agitated. She could see her agent and the producer arguing later.

While shooting the last few scenes, she got a call from another producer; he wanted her and only her to play in an autobiography about Judy Garland. Melissa unofficially accepted, pending the contract and review of the script. This time she would review the contract and script herself. This was going to be a great "one-two" punch for her career. Beach Daze was an in-depth romance with a side dish of suspense and mystery. Now she was going to be playing one of Hollywood's most iconic actresses. She had been nominated for Oscars before, but she felt that if she played Judy well on the heels of playing Madison, she would maybe be in the running again.

Leaving Hawaii was bittersweet; she really liked it here and was considering buying a vacation home here. Instead, she secretly paid the college tuition of the waitress that helped her at the restaurant and bought her a new car. Her agent wanted to announce it publicly, but Melissa didn't want the recognition; she just wanted to help, as the waitress had helped her.

Just as she did with Madison, Melissa took on all aspects of Judy's life, even going as far as smoking a few cigarettes just to get the experience. She stayed clear of the other drugs and moderated her alcohol intake. She started copying her Midwest accent and watched all of Judy's movies. She went to Judy's hometown and talked with those close to her when she was a child. She had her hair colored to match Judy's, which was helpful in avoiding the media. Then came the dresses; many of the dresses Judy had worn in movies and out at awards had been replicated and fit to Melissa. The most notable was the green velvet dress from "Easter Parade." Though she had been taking singing lessons, this part really pushed her to the next level, so much so that her agent was asking about possibly recording an album when she was done with the movie. Melissa didn't like that but did agree to record a few singles for the soundtrack.

After this movie was over, she wanted to take it easy—maybe just do some cameo appearances on daytime TV. She liked how Julia Roberts had been on Law & Order and how James Earl Jones and Carrie Fisher appeared in The Big Bang Theory.

The producer wanted to have a big party at the release of the film. Melissa was already fatigued from filming two movies within a year and a half and didn't want to go, but her agent was insistent. Janet, her agent, had been acting very odd lately, asking Melissa for a higher commission and even asking for a couple of advances in payment. At the party, she felt very tired and was getting very paranoid of one photographer in particular who seemed to be following her; he even went as far as talking to her agent.

"Janet, I need to go; I have a huge headache, and I am tired. I couldn't even finish my wine."

"Here, take this and have some water. You will be just fine," Janet said as she passed a pill to Melissa.

"What is this?"

"Oh, it's just some really strong headache medicine. Go out to your car, get some air, and then you will be feeling right as rain."

Melissa grabbed a glass of water from a tray, took the pill, and headed to her car. As she walked, her vision started to get blurry, and she felt even more tired. She got her keys out of her purse and opened the door to her Mercedes. She could hear her pulse in her ears now. She sat down in the driver's seat but flopped over the console, leaving her legs out of the car and the door open. Her vision went from blurry to dim to dark. Did her eyes close, or did she just go blind?

THERE SHE WAS, THERE FOR the taking. The money he had paid her agent had been worth it. Nobody was back here; if she screamed, she would get people's attention, but she was in no shape to do that. He walked over like a spilled ooze creeping across a floor. Her dress was short and would make his job easy. He had his plan mapped out; nude pictures of Melissa Andrews would sell for millions of dollars. He had a cash cow passed out right in front of him, not even including the money she would pay to make the pictures stop. Her underwear would be worth a lot too.

He reached up to pull off her underwear, but she was still bearing on them. No matter, he would just pull harder; they would either slide off or tear off.

Melissa could feel something—something wrong, something off. Somebody's hands, strange hands; she felt a sharp tugging at her waist like something was trying to cut into her skin. She opened her eyes just to see her keys in her hand and a red button labeled panic; at the same time, the cutting feeling got worse. She pushed the red button on her key fob; the first blast of the horn startled her; it woke her up a little. She picked her head up to see the photographer pulling his hands and camera out from under her dress. Her purse was still in her other hand, so she did all she could do and started flailing the purse at the man like a weapon. She wasn't sure what was in her purse, but it was working. She had no real aim, but she managed to land some blows, then her other arm came into the fray and started hitting the man with her keys as well. The horn honking in repetition had attracted onlookers; unfortunately, their timing was off, and to them it just looked like Melissa was beating the heck out of a photographer.

The police showed up and asked what happened. The photographer's story was that he had found Ms. Andrews drunk and high, wandering around and trying to get in her car. He was trying to help her into the car and take her keys. Considering Melissa's side of the story, which was foggy at best, they allowed the photographer to walk away with no charges. The photographer chose not to press charges against Ms. Andrews, figuring an investigation into the real events would not go well for him or Melissa's agent. Maureen arrived and took Melissa home.

The next morning, the trial began—the trial by social media and public opinion. All footage of the incident from onlookers made the photographer look like the victim and made it look like Melissa Andrews was drunk and high on drugs and having a fit at some good Samaritan. Melissa's agent told her that the publicity would blow over and, in a month or two, it would be no big deal. Melissa, already strained after the back-to-back movies, now felt more stress from this incident. She wanted to get away; she wanted to be by the ocean. She started looking at places she could hide. Going back to Hawaii was out of the question, as everyone would recognize her there, but she knew she wanted to be by the ocean. She slid the cursor on her laptop across the country from the west coast to the east.

She started googling different locations, murmuring to herself, "North Carolina, Virginia, Jersey, Massachusetts, ahh, Maine. Now a quiet town on the coast, but not too far from civilization."

CHAPTER NINE
Boothbay Harbor

BOOTHBAY HARBOR WAS A SMALL town on the coast of Maine. Although the population almost tripled in the summer, it was mostly from tourists. Tourists were a good thing; she could blend in and hide in plain sight. Knowing that her credit card wouldn't go unnoticed and she didn't want her agent involved, she decided to involve her housekeeper, Maureen. Maureen and Melissa worked together and scheduled the private jet; she had often contemplated getting her own jet, but that seemed a bit over the top to her. They had arranged for a rental car, a Ford Focus sedan, to be left at the Brunswick Executive Airport. From there, it would be a forty-five-minute drive to Boothbay Harbor and the rental cabin that would be her home for a while. The jet, car, and cabin were all paid for using a credit card in Maureen's name.

She didn't even tell her agent where she was going; she just told her she was leaving and not to schedule anything for her. The flight was uneventful; she slept through most of it, and when she wasn't asleep, she was reading. She and Maureen had timed the flight to land in Brunswick at night so there would be fewer people there. She was wearing a simple T-shirt and jeans and a ball cap, an outfit she donned many times to avoid reporters. She wasn't even wearing any makeup.

After the plane had landed and the door was opened, the first smells of Maine brushed her senses. Even here at this small airport of sorts, the smell of fresh, clean air filled her lungs; she took a deep breath and held it in and closed her eyes to let it soak in. She was free—free of Hollywood, free of her agent, free of the ominous media. She opened her eyes and looked out, looking for the rental car that would take her to her retreat.

The sight of the little car made her smile; it was relatively the same size as her Mercedes AMG GT, but it didn't look like it was going to eat the road for breakfast. The differences in the car became more apparent once she got in. Not only did the door "clunk" when shut, but the seat reminded her of the public transportation bus seats they had used in filming; the seat did not hug her like her Mercedes did. The interior was dramatically different, much more utilitarian and plastic than the leather and carbon fiber of her GT. She wasn't annoyed in the least; she wanted to leave Hollywood behind, and this was a good first step. She typed in the address to the navigation app on her smartphone and got on her way. Again, once driving, the difference between her Mercedes and the Ford was more apparent, which was probably a good thing. She needed to lay low, and getting a speeding ticket would not be the best way to do that.

Not long after she pulled away from the airport, Melissa felt hungry. It was late, and she really didn't feel like eating in a restaurant even if she could find one that was open, not to mention she didn't want to take the risk of being recognized. She saw a McDonald's up ahead and laughed out loud. Yes, Melissa Andrews, who normally dined at five-star restaurants and had a chef at her mansion, would now be eating fast food. She told herself not to make it a habit; it was one of the reasons she chose Boothbay Harbor; there were no fast-food restaurants in town.

It occurred to her that this would be her first time going through a drive-thru. The ordering felt awkward; she had driven up to the speaker and had no idea what she was going to order. All she knew was she was hungry; she looked quickly at the menu, then picked a Big Mac with cheese, fries, and a medium Coke. She realized she had no cash on her, so she used a credit card, fearing the person would see the name Melissa Andrews, but to her relief, the cashier swiped the card and passed it back without an issue. At the next window, she was given her food and drink, and she was on her way. The aroma wafted through the car, making her hunger even worse. Her original plan was to eat while driving, but after one look at the burger, she decided against it. She pulled over in a well-lit parking lot and began to eat.

The burger tasted good, but she could tell that the meat and cheese were processed, and they just felt wrong. If she were not so hungry, she would never have been able to eat it. This felt almost cozy in a way in this little car, lit by streetlights and the ambient light of the dashboard. It was the beginning of June, so the night air wasn't warm but cold enough to justify putting the heat on low in the car, and she felt the warm air as it hit the tops of her feet. She was surprised at herself that she had finished the burger, then her stomach reassured her that she had in fact finished it. She decided to get driving again and to snack on the fries while driving; even though she was full, she couldn't help but eat the fries. She would never dream of eating in her Mercedes.

She soon made the turn from Route One to Route Twenty-seven; she was closer now. The winding road made her miss her Mercedes more and more. She passed a Welcome to Boothbay sign, and that made her curious about the difference between Boothbay and Boothbay Harbor; maybe she could look that up during her visit. She found herself slowing down and taking in the scenery; this was much different than what she was used to. So many trees with houses tucked neatly inside of them, small businesses and shops, all weaved into the natural surroundings, not industrial or cluttered. She passed a large common with a small stand that advertised "Free Beer Tomorrow," and it made her laugh. Then there was the Welcome to Boothbay Harbor sign; she was almost there. She had noticed, starting way back in Edgecomb, that the towns had flags with the pictures and names of the service members hung on the telephone poles. She felt it was a great way to honor those that had served.

She turned the heat up a little more and cracked open her window. The smell of the processed dinner was soon replaced with the smell of the ocean. It smelled different than it did in Hawaii, but she knew it had to be the ocean. She took several long, deep breaths of it, as if it were a drug—a clean drug with no high, just an odor that made you feel good. She was confused for a moment when it seemed that the GPS wanted her to go down a one-way street, but after careful inspection, she determined Pear Street was two-way. At the end of Pear Street, just to the left side of a restaurant named Brady's, she could see the glittering surface of the water. As she took the left indicated by the GPS app, she found it hard to focus on where she was going and not on the water. She could see the footbridge she had read about and couldn't wait to walk over it. Maybe she would even get lunch somewhere and eat it right there on the bridge. The ocean smell was more prevalent now. She kept looking over the harbor while driving down Atlantic Avenue. She was coming up to her next turn, a left onto Lobster Cove Road. Before that turn, there was a beautiful church that overlooked the harbor.

The next turn was a left onto Crest Avenue; now she was surrounded by trees. "No wonder they call this place Sprucewold," she said out loud. She carefully kept an eye on her GPS while looking at the little green street names with reflective lettering. It was a little confusing because Crest Avenue kept going to the right, and she had to veer left to go on Nahanada Road. She found herself repeating "Nahanada" several times because it was fun to say. She was starting to become a little giddy with this independence. No agent was around; she was really on her own. Then Nahanada Road turned into Birch Road. She slowed down and looked at the house numbers. At first all she could see was a driveway with a post and the number on it, but when she turned into the driveway, a small two-car spot, the headlights revealed a small path and the roof of a small cabin. She sighed in relief; she had made it. Now, had they remembered to leave a key? She grabbed her suitcase out of the back and walked down the small path.

It was just as the pictures showed, although in the dark she couldn't see much detail. A simple brown log cabin nestled in surrounding spruce trees. Just as it said in the email, the key was underneath the welcome mat. She unlocked and opened the door while taking in a deep breath of air. The cabin smelled of spruce and cedar, with a hint of the salty air from outside. There was a welcome letter on the table, which she chose to ignore for now. She just wanted sleep for right now; it was approaching midnight, and her mind and body said it was time to sleep. She opened her suitcase just to pull out some shorts and a T-shirt to sleep in. She went up the stairs to the bedroom and crawled under the covers. She glanced at her phone briefly, considering setting an alarm. No, she wanted to sleep in; she would let her body and mind wake up when they were ready.

She opened her eyes the next morning feeling much better than she had in a while, as if breathing the fresh Maine air overnight had healed all the damage caused by the stress of the past few weeks. She looked at her phone and saw it was nine forty-eight; she had slept almost a full ten hours; it was time to get this hiatus moving. She sat up and looked out the window only to see a light gray fog that the sun was trying to burn through. There were sounds of birds chirping outside, so she opened her window and found the air just slightly cold against her skin, but with the fog, she knew it would be warmer soon.

She took a shower, unpacked her belongings, and made herself at home. She looked at the coffee maker but decided against attempting to make coffee; there would be time for that later. She searched the cupboards and found they were stocked with a few items. She found some English muffins, and, in the refrigerator, there was some locally made blueberry jam. She knew how to operate a toaster, so she settled for an English muffin and some tea as a small breakfast. She would need a little fuel, as she intended to go for a walk soon. She really wanted to walk across that footbridge and check out the stores on the other side. She also wanted to burn off that Big Mac and fries from last night. While she ate, she took in the sounds around her. There were boats out on the water all motoring around, seagulls cackling, and squirrels calling to each other. This place was already functioning as she had hoped.

She laced up her sneakers and thought about putting her earbuds in but decided to take in more of the soundtrack that Boothbay Harbor had to offer. She started on her way with the destination of the footbridge in mind. The walk started all downhill, which delivered a steady workout to the back of her calves. She kept a steady pace while she made the turn onto Lobster Cove Road. An older gentleman in an old Chevy pickup who was smoking a pipe gave her a wave as he drove by; she returned the wave in kind.

She watched the truck go down the road and heard the truck honk its horn, and the driver waved to someone at the house on the left. Was this normal? Most people where she was from didn't wave when they honked their horns; usually it was a middle finger followed by some profanity. As she walked closer to the end of Lobster Cove Road, she saw whom the man in the truck waved to. An older bearded man was outside; his hair and beard were all white, which gave him the appearance of Santa Claus, minus the red suit. He looked as if he were measuring rope with his arms. Once he counted so many arm lengths, he tied the end of the rope to one of the neatly stacked green cages that were lined up beside his driveway.

"Good morning," she called to the man without even thinking about it. It was like the air here or the friendly aura of this place made her do it.

The older man looked up and said, "Good morning," and Melissa had to fight the urge to laugh when it looked as if the man had lost count of his arm lengths.

The church she had seen on the way in looked much larger in the daylight. The golden cross at the top seemed to look out over the harbor, as if to keep an eye on it. It had to be one of the most beautiful buildings she had ever seen. She was not religious, but she had to appreciate the work that must have gone into building such a place and the effort it took to keep it so gorgeous. She stopped to take a picture without even knowing why.

She noticed a memorial she had missed on the way in, the Lost at Sea memorial. She would have to stop one of these days and check it out. Out on the harbor there were more boats motoring around; she had read a little about the lobstering industry and how it was Boothbay Harbor's biggest staple, much like the rest of the coast of Maine. She could see the bridge now; she was closing in. Soon she found herself at the beginning of the bridge; she had no idea why it drew her in or why she was so fascinated by it, but she enjoyed every step she took, smiling at people as they walked by. Nobody seemed to recognize her in her "street" clothes of sunglasses and ball cap. She was just another tourist out for a walk. When she was at the halfway point, she stopped and looked out over the harbor and made a mental list of other things to do —a whale-watching trip, a cruise of the inner harbor, and taking a walk at nighttime.

At the end of the footbridge, she took a left; there was a bowling alley to the left, then a saltwater taffy store, then an ice cream store. All these little stores and shops just felt so quaint and humble. She loved it. She looked around at her surroundings, and she noticed a store just up the hill. "Sherman's Bookstore," she said out loud to herself. "Bingo," she added. She could not remember the last time she just sat down and read a book. She marched up the hill to the store to find the door propped open. As she walked in, the ladies behind the counter greeted her warmly. She saw the store was so much bigger on the inside than she anticipated. She stood in awe, taking it all in.

Another employee with a name tag that said "Debbie" and an accent she couldn't place came up to her. "Can I help you find something?"

"Ah yes, I am on vacation." Melissa had to laugh at the statement; practically everyone here was on vacation. "I am looking to soak up some Maine culture."

"Oh, we have this table here with all Maine authors." Debbie said as she pointed to a table in the middle, just inside the entrance.

"Thank you; that is perfect."

"Let me know if you need anything else."

Melissa looked at the table; she recognized Stephen King's name, but she wasn't interested in horror. She listed off the names in her head: "Paul Doiron, Linda Greenlaw, Jerry Farnham..."

SHE LEFT SHERMAN'S WITH A bag full of books to read and continued down the sidewalk, sometimes crossing the street, bouncing in and out of several stores. She had to remember she was walking home and would be carrying everything. When lunchtime rolled around, she got a takeout order of haddock tacos from Kalers and took it to the footbridge to eat.

After lunch, she walked back to her cabin for a nap. She woke up late in the afternoon and decided it was time to go grocery shopping. She would get takeout from Brady's for dinner that night as well.

The Hannaford grocery store was an interesting experience; not only was she grocery shopping for the first time but listening to the conversations was an experience as well. These people were so friendly, not only to each other but to her, a stranger, as well. People were saying "hello" and smiling. People were saying "excuse me" to get by. It was like she was in a movie set from the nineteen fifties, but she wasn't—this was real; they were real.

After dinner, she decided to take a walk to Barrett's Park. She met an old, bearded man walking his dog, Blueberry. She had to listen hard because he seemed to talk fast and in a high pitch. She learned his name was Everett Trask, and he had grown up in the area.

Melissa got in the habit of getting up early and watching the lobster boats leaving the cove nearby. There were two, a smaller black one and a larger red one. She didn't know why, but she was drawn to the red one. She had only seen the occupant briefly, but he was good-looking. Then in the afternoon she would see them return. She had watched the two in the black boat haul up a trap. She wondered how the older one could talk and not lose his pipe overboard. She never could seem to catch the red one hauling by the dock.

Along with the boat watching, she had started a routine of running. She had learned she didn't really know how to cook anything other than spaghetti or macaroni and cheese from a box or other prepared meals, so she found herself getting takeout a lot. Running helped her stay in shape. It was also like meditation—reflecting on her life and what she had done. After her run, it was tourist time. She would pick a local tourist attraction and go visit it. She loved the whale watch and had even seen her red lobster boat while out. She greatly enjoyed the Maine Botanical Gardens and sent pictures to Maureen to give to the gardener. The aquarium was a fun visit, and she learned more of what Maine was about. Some nights she would stay in and just read one of her books; other nights she would hang out at the waterfront, just observing people. Not to mention the conversations she had with Everett and Blueberry.

Boothbay Harbor had turned out to be just the medicine she needed. It had character, a slow pace, and everyone was friendly. From the early mornings of listening to the lobster boats leave the nearby cove, to her evenings being entertained by the birds, squirrels, and chipmunks, she felt like she was healing; not just from the most recent of events, but from a lifetime of going full speed and never really taking care of herself.

PART THREE
RED AT NIGHT

ONE MORNING, MELISSA DECIDED IT was time to get out on the water. She also wanted to possibly find that red lobster boat she had been seeing; she had seen it go by earlier that morning. Much like the footbridge on her first day here, she found herself attracted to the operator. She also had set the goal of paddling across the bay because it didn't look that far, and she had been running to stay in shape. She did put on her wetsuit; she was glad she packed it. She took a kayak off the rack and grabbed a paddle. She set her sights on the shore across the bay, all while looking for the red boat. She paddled slowly, conserving her energy and taking in the sights.

She passed Cabbage Island on her right, and a resort of sorts was to her left. She kept an easy pace, enjoying the serenity of the ocean. She also started realizing that she greatly underestimated the distance, but she would not be discouraged; she had all day. As she got closer to the other side of the bay, the wind started picking up. She noticed she was fighting the wind more as the chop was getting more aggressive, and her arms were feeling tired. She saw a small beach she could pull up on and rest for a moment; then she saw it—the red boat. It was a distance away, but it was getting closer. She had paid so much attention to the red boat that she didn't notice the white boat going by and pulling a large wake. By the time she saw the wake, it was too late. The kayak rolled, dumping her into the water.

Jack Finn had just pulled away from having a quick break with his father. He was looking forward to hanging out on the dock tonight; he just had to avoid the questions of when he would be seeing someone again. He wasn't ready for that yet; he wasn't sure he would ever be ready. His mother and Lucy knew better than to push the issue, and the same with his dad, but that wouldn't stop some of the local girls from trying to push him. "What the hell am I going on about?" he said to himself. "Just enjoy the day, and whatever happens, happens." Before turning for his next buoy, he glanced forward, just off his bow, to see a young woman in a kayak not far in the distance, and not far from the kayak was Dale Rines.

Dale Rines was in a foul mood; he had run out of money, so he had to come out and haul traps today to try and make some. He had gotten to the dock late that morning, and the only bait they had was some rancid redfish that had maggots in it. Luckily for him, the wind had picked up and was blowing the stench away. Not so lucky for him; since it had been so long since he hauled his traps, he wasn't even getting a pound per trap. He took another long haul from the Gatorade and vodka mix he had sitting on the dash of his boat; it was warm, but at least it was wet. He had no other vices on him, but he was sure his friend Tommy would have something for him when he went in to sell.

HE COULD SEE JACK FINN in his fancy red boat hauling behind him. Man, did he hate Jack; he was such a goody-two-shoes. Jack always had the best stuff, too. In high school, he had the fastest skiff; then he started dating Stephanie Turner; then he got that truck. Dale couldn't figure out how he did it either. The more he looked back at Jack, the angrier he got. He looked ahead to see a young woman kayaking.

"OOOhhhh, look at what we have here," he said, checking out what he could see of the young woman. "You look a little tired, sweetheart. Let me help you out of that kayak, and I can come back and save you, then... you can thank me, whether you want to or not."

Dale proceeded with his half-conceived plan to roll the young lady's kayak over and then, when she was floundering, go back and help her out of the water. She already looked tired; she wouldn't be able to put up much of a fight. He throttled up to make the biggest wake possible and looked back at the kayaker to make sure she fell out. He saw Jack was facing the other way, in the middle of hauling a pair of traps.

"Bullseye!" he exclaimed as the boat wake rolled the kayak over, but in his state of not paying attention, he had run over a couple of buoys. His boat was now making a loud grumbling sound from the bottom, and it shook violently.

"FUCK...fuck, fuck, fuck," He screamed out loud. "Fucking rope in the wheel!"

He looked back to see the *Red at Night*, with Jack pulling the young lady from the water.

Glossary

IN THIS INSTALLMENT THERE IS some Navy terminology.

- Petty Officer Second Class: This is an E-5 in the US Navy

- Master Chief Petty Officer or Master Chief: This is an E-9 in the US Navy, the highest enlisted rank

- EN2-Engineerman 2nd Class: A Petty Officer Second Class with the Engineman designation

- QM3: Quartermaster 3rd Class: A Petty Officer Third Class with a Quartermaster designation.

- Exfil- Exfiltration or exit point in a military operation.

JERRY learning the craft from his Dad

About the Author

I was raised in Boothbay Harbor, the son of a lobsterman. I grew up on a lobster boat going sternman every summer from age six until I left to serve my country in the US Navy.

I returned to civilian life in 2007, taking several jobs and going back to school before settling in Gorham, Maine, with my wife and 2 kids. I enjoy writing, unprofessionally, for Downeast Boat Forum (www.DowneastBoatForum.com), archery, spending time on the water, or tinkering with my Jeep named MeatLug, and most of all I love being a husband and father.

Connect with me online:

http://www.jerryfarnham.com/